PURSUIT

Center Point
Large Print

Also by Joyce Carol Oates and available from Center Point Large Print:

Dis Mem Ber
The Doll-Master
Jack of Spades
Night-Gaunts

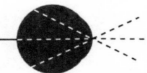

**This Large Print Book carries the
Seal of Approval of N.A.V.H.**

PURSUIT

A Novel of Suspense

Joyce Carol Oates

CENTER POINT LARGE PRINT
THORNDIKE, MAINE

This Center Point Large Print edition
is published in the year 2020 by arrangement with
The Mysterious Press, an imprint of Grove Atlantic.

The text of this Large Print edition is unabridged.
In other aspects, this book may vary
from the original edition.
Printed in the United States of America
on permanent paper.
Set in 16-point Times New Roman type.

ISBN: 978-1-64358-487-4

The Library of Congress has cataloged this record
under Library of Congress Control Number: 2019951752

PURSUIT

for Arthur Vanderbilt

The Young Husband

*What were you telling yourself when it happened?
You have to remember.*

*I think you know. I think you must tell me. For
both of us, you have to remember and to speak
truly.*

That moment. Just before it happened.

We need to return to that moment.

*When you left the bus. When you stood on the
curb.*

When you stepped off the curb.

If you did it accidentally, or—deliberately.

We need to pursue this. We need to know.

*Your lung has been punctured. Your collarbone
and five ribs were broken.*

*Your skull has a half a dozen hairline frac-
tures. Your brain has been bruised, lacerated.
The danger is blood clots in the heart.*

*You seemed to be "deciding something"—the
bus driver said.*

*We need to return to that moment. We need to
know why.*

*Why you did what you did, what you were
telling yourself when it happened. When you
stepped off the curb.*

The morning after our wedding day.

Skeleton Dance

Skel-e-ton. Pressing her face into the pillow she whispers the (dread) word (just barely) aloud.

Uncertain what *skeleton* means, exactly. Though (maybe) she knows what it means.

Skel-e-ton. Skele-ton. Skeleton.

A terrible (adult) word not to be said aloud. A word that a child would not know, and certainly a child would not utter. A word that, the more you utter it, the more terrible it becomes. A word that fascinates, like a poisonous vapor lifting to your nostrils, which you know you should not inhale and yet—you cannot resist inhaling.

This recurring dream she has while growing up. After her parents disappear. After she is living with relatives.

Skeletons. In the grassy place.

So many times this dream. Virtually every night. In the places where people take her. Her things crammed into what is called a bed-pack.

Shivering so that her teeth chatter like castanets.

Yes, sometimes in this new place she wets the bed, she is so frightened. The murmured words *wets the bed* will shame and torment her through her life.

Can't comprehend who it is, what it is, that forces her to run along the overgrown path. Forces her to stagger through the tall grasses that tear at her hands, her face. Forces her to *see.*

Did you think you could forget us? Did you think we could forget you?

It was a time long ago. If there was a road from this-time to that-time, there'd be a break in the road, a collapse, so you'd have to climb down inside the collapsed road to get across. It was that far away.

In that time long ago, the terrible dream of the skeletons.

So many times she'd had the dream. Rippling through her small body like an electric current waking her instantaneously.

Shivering with cold. Not enough breath to scream.

You could tell—the skulls.

(Human) skulls. Not animal.

In the tall grasses. By the creek.

Didn't see closely. No.

But—you did see. Shut your eyes too late.

Seeing that one skull was bigger than the other, this was the Daddy-skull. The smaller skull was the Mommy-skull.

In the tall grasses the bones were scattered together so it looked (almost) as if they were dancing. Lying down where they'd fallen a long time ago.

Wedding Morning

*Did you think you could forget us? Did you think
we would forget you?*

Early on the morning of her wedding day. Before
dawn she is wakened from the dream with a jolt.
The skeleton dream she had reason to believe
she'd outgrown, vivid before her staring eyes.

Bathed in sweat inside the white cotton nightgown. The last time she will be wearing this
(threadbare, favorite) nightgown with the lace
trim, as it is the last time she will be sleeping
alone.

Yes, she is (still) a virgin. At least there is that.

Exhausted and stunned, lying on her back in
a place that feels churned, rutted like earth, but
is her bed. Her skin is chafed as if sharp grass
blades have whipped against it. In the dream,
she has been running, desperate and panting for
breath, though the logic of the dream tells her
that it is futile to run.

Did you think you could escape us?

Not knowing at first where she is or what time
this is, for in the terrible dream she is very young
and in a place not this place in that long-ago time.

This self she has carefully constructed as an
adult among the adults of the world—this being
does not yet exist in the dream. In the dream there

is only the child-self, her truest self, unprotected, as a newborn deer is unprotected, lacking even a scent.

Unprotected as a child whose mother has abandoned her.

Unprotected as a child taken into the home of an aunt out of pity after her parents have abandoned her.

In her sleep she'd sensed that it was imminent, the skeleton dream. For first there is the premonition, a feeling of paralysis in her limbs and numbness in her being, an anticipation of something very terrible at which you must not look, yet in the dream you must look for you have no choice.

But why on her wedding eve? Why this old, terrible dream of childhood . . .

She is in the grassy place by the shallow creek. Litter has been swept downstream by rainstorms, flooding. Pieces of debris, broken tree limbs, mummified bodies of small animals. Remains of a rotted backpack. And among these objects, scattered in the grass, the skeletons.

How would you know that the bones are human bones?—You would not.

She does not. No!

Except for the skulls. Near hidden in the grass, not far apart. Waiting for her.

The larger skull with gaping eye sockets, nose. Grinning broken teeth in an unhinged jaw for he'd been shouting.

The smaller skull, with smaller eye sockets, nose. This is the quiet skull, the watchful and wary skull.

It is significant, unless it is purely chance, that each skull has come to rest faceup.

Whoever she is in the dream is not who she is now. No longer.

Much older now. Twenty years old now.

Safe! An adult.

Except: observing the creek bed, the glittering water. If you listen closely, you can hear. Voices, just audible. *Meer-me! Meer-me!*

A scattering of large rocks, boulders. Some have been bleached bone-white by the sun. Some are dull gray, leaden. Some are covered with curious, gnarled growths, like tumors. A few of the bones have made their way into the streambed, carried a little distance downstream, lodged in rocks, as if they'd sought to escape and had failed.

How long ago, the living flesh had died, turned rancid, melted, and fallen from the bones . . .

Clavicle. Humerus. Femur. Tibia. Carpals. Ribs. Sternum . . . How is it that she knows the names of these bones? She has never taken a course in biology. She has no aptitude for science.

Her fiancé would know the names of bones. Premed at the state university. Though he has become discouraged by the cutthroat competition in the program, which leaves him trailing behind a third of the class, not willing to cheat even if he'd been capable of cheating with the expertise and panache of the other students. *Maybe I just don't want to be a doctor that badly. D'you mind, Abby? Not being a doctor's wife?*

She'd laughed, and kissed him. So grateful to her fiancé for loving her without knowing what festers in her heart, she'd have forgiven him anything.

The Bride

Blinding bright April morning of a lost year. Has she been married just *one day?*

To be precise, at this hour of the morning (8:11 a.m.) she has been married just twenty-one hours.

The wonder of it takes her breath away. The shock of it.

Oh, has this happened to me? Married.

Needing to be alone on the Raritan Avenue bus taking her into downtown Hammond, she hoped to sit by herself at the rear. The wonder of *married . . . wife . . .* she wants to contemplate alone.

For at age twenty she has a sweet guileless pale-freckled face that makes strangers want to talk to her. Smile at her. *Hel-lo! Gosh-darn cold this morning isn't it?*—and she is too polite to turn away, too shy not to respond, and there she'd be: her solitude on the bus ruined.

First morning of her married life, so precious. In dread of someone intruding.

D'you take this bus often, miss? I think I've seen you . . .

No. No.

Maybe at the movies? You go to the movies? Last Friday—did you? Could swear I'd seen you . . . Hey: you look like you could be in the movies, like what's-her-name . . .

No. Not.

Except you're better-looking than she is. Younger.

Like the filament in a lightbulb, glowing. Within. Her happiness at being married to a good, kind, decent man she loves, who adores her.

But it is a private happiness. She wants to cup it in both hands like a flame, to shield it from the wind.

Is that a wedding band? Hey—you're somebody's wife?

Excuse me for being nosy—but—you don't look old enough to be anybody's wife . . . Eh?

Don't look older 'n—what?—sixteen.

Nervous smile. Always polite. Avoiding eyes. Unconscious habit, rubbing her left wrist.

Circling her left wrist is a red, rashlike mark. As if her wrist has been tied, tightly. And the rope, or twine, has been scraped against her sensitive skin, rubbing it raw in places.

(As a girl you learn not to offend strangers by rebuffing them. Especially men. Strangers, but also employers. And, when she'd been a student for what had seemed like forever, teachers. Smiling and friendly-seeming because you are pretty but if you say the wrong words or fail to smile with the expected vivacity, a man can turn nasty. Fast.)

Well—have a great day, sweetheart! This is my stop.

Two unoccupied seats at the rear, and cleverly

she sits in the outer seat, leaving the inner seat beside the window unoccupied. So it isn't convenient for anyone to stumble over her feet to sit there. If anyone wants to sit with her, they must ask her to move over, which she will do (of course) but with an air of distraction, as if her thoughts are elsewhere.

Not practiced in being married, for it is not yet a full day that she has been Mrs. Willem Zengler, but she is practiced in avoiding the eyes of strangers in public places. Even friendly-seeming women.

Excuse me, miss—is that seat occupied?

Has to say no. Not occupied.

Has to move over, beside the window. Stiff smile, turn to the window, hide her left hand with the silver wedding band.

Cold this morning isn't it! Damn wind waiting for the damn bus . . .

Pretending not to hear. At County Services you encounter deaf persons, some of them just teenagers, children. It is not so uncommon to be hearing impaired.

She has worked with the blind, also. Sight impaired.

She wonders if there is a classification for *soul impaired.*

Still, the person beside her continues to talk to her, or rather toward her. Somebody's old Elmer Fudd daddy. Talking to himself, complaining, but in a humorous way, in the hope that the pretty, freckled girl beside him will overhear something interesting and respond with a giggle, a flirtatious sidelong glance.

She has not seen who it is. She will not turn to him even with a sigh of exasperation, though (damn him) he has begun to spread his weight, his bulk, into the hard plastic seat that is her seat, inconspicuously, as if he has been holding his breath and is now releasing it.

Too bad her tall handsome young husband isn't with her this morning. Close beside her. Gripping her hand in his. Willem would protect her with his life. (She knew.)

No one could sit beside her if Willem were here. Intrude upon her private happiness.

But Willem has taken another bus, to another part of the city. Willem on his way to the university.

Oh, the first morning of being Mrs. Willem Zengler! Her new life.

The newlyweds have not enough money for anything like a honeymoon just yet. They must both work, and Willem has classes. Early Saturday morning they will drive north to Lake George to stay in a cabin borrowed from a friend of Willem's father; Sunday night they will drive home. When they have a three-day weekend, possibly they'll see Niagara Falls, which is just five hours away.

But someday they will have a real honeymoon, in a romantic place like Miami Beach or Paris. Willem has promised.

Beside her, the heavyset stranger's thigh presses against hers. Through layers of clothing, even her coat, the pressure is insistent.

Shrinks from him. Trying to be unobtrusive.

It is possible that the man's bulk easing into her seat is accidental. No doubt he is simply a heavy man. And old. She can hear him breathing, an asthmatic wheeze.

Perhaps he is offended by her reticence. The rambling talk has ceased.

But the strain has made her anxious. She is keenly sensitive to the moods of adults, especially adult males.

How swiftly the mood can change. In an instant, the mood can change. The signal is a stiffness in the jaws. Tendons in the neck. Intake of breath.

Come here. Where d'you think you are going?
Here. Right here. I said—

(But why is she thinking these upsetting thoughts? On this morning of all mornings!)

So badly she'd wanted to be alone with her newfound happiness. First morning of married life. First morning of the rest of her life—Mrs. Willem Zengler.

How *Zengler* swallows up *Hayman*. So grateful!

Everyone on the bus would smile at Mrs. Zengler if they knew. How she would blush, if they knew. Jokes about honeymoons, wedding nights—she just doesn't hear, does not think such jokes are funny.

This precious morning, prized in secret as the lumbering Raritan Avenue bus bears her downtown to County Services. If the man beside her has decided to leave her alone, she is safe to recall her happiness.

Giddy blur of joy, relief, gratitude. Her wedding day.

(Frankly, she had not expected it to happen. Had been sure that something terrible would prevent it.)

(The worst thing now in her life would be Willem's death. Because she loves him so. Her own death, not much. Just an erasure.)

All the wedding guests were the bridegroom's, and there were not many of these. The bride's relatives lived too far away to attend. Could not afford to travel. Obscurely it was believed that the bride was *adopted,* in any case.

She wonders if the Zenglers are suspicious of her. In their place, she would be.

But then she is always suspicious of smiling people.

Skel-e-ton. Skeleton!

In a rush, like bile at the back of her mouth, the memory comes. The dream . . .

Previous morning, before the wedding. Waking before dawn, frightened and shaking, her nightgown soaked with sweat.

Smelling of her body. That shameful smell.

Her fear is—now that she is married and can

no longer sleep alone—that she will wake stammering and whimpering from that dream, or from another. And Willem will see for the first time her face contorted with fear.

Fear makes a pretty face ugly. Always, hide your fear.

Always hide your weakness, as animals do.

Fortunately, all she can remember of the wedding night is a blur of (drunken) happiness. Too long she'd been a virgin, and too long her ardent young Christian husband had been "waiting" for her, as he'd said, half in complaint and half in pride, for he was a serious Christian. His family were Methodists and did not believe in what was (quaintly) called *premarital sex.*

Sure, he'd said. A guy puts pressure on a girl, especially his fiancée, like he's in pain, suffering, but secretly he doesn't want her to give in.

Give in. She is listening closely.

Because—d'you know why?

She tells him no. Why?

(Of course she knows why! What a joke.)

If a girl is "easy," it means she might be "easy" with other men. Earnestly Willem explains.

As earnestly she has heard Willem explain that his name is not *William.* It is *Willem.*

Who'd told him this, the fiancée wondered. Who tells boys these things about girls? About women?

Presumably older boys. Willem has brothers, cousins.

Nice Christian boys but still, they have dirty minds like most other guys. At least the normal ones.

She is not proud of the fact, but she has deceived Willem Zengler many times. Even before they'd become engaged.

Not with other men. Not with boys. Rather, she has deceived Willem as she has deceived others by hiding from them the true nature of her soul, which is stained, discolored, as foul as a filthy sponge.

Any bad thing that happens to me, I deserve.

No good thing that happens to me, do I deserve.

Telling Willem that her name was Abby—that is, Gabriella, shortened to Abby.

Her real name, her legal name, the name on her birth certificate is nothing like Abby *or* Gabriella. For some reason she can't name, she will introduce herself as Abby to individuals her own age who she is hoping will like her.

The birth certificate name is Miriam Frances Hayman. Not *her.*

She and Willem met at County Services, where she was working in the Rehabilitation Center for the Blind. Willem had been one of a dozen Christian Youth volunteers who'd come to the center once a week to read to the people there.

Hadn't liked him at first. Hadn't wanted to like him. Just a glance at him—tall, blond, "boyish" handsome, kindly blue eyes—something inside her panicked. Shrank, curled up like a worm to protect itself.

Sex-desire. Any kind of quick jolt of emotion. Belly, heart. Brings tears to the eyes. *No.*

Shameless but funny, she supposes, how certain of her (female) coworkers managed to cross paths with Willem Zengler as frequently as they could. The Rehabilitation Center was located on the first floor of the County Services building, not far from a women's lavatory. Convenient!

Certain (married) women who should have known better, drifting about the corridors in the hope of encountering the tall, blond Christian Youth volunteer who greeted them like a gentleman, though he was just a kid in his mid-twenties, if not younger.

Even the rehab supervisor (had to be fifty years old) waylaying him with cheery remarks and questions—shameless.

Even blind women seemed to catch on. Maybe they sniffed something. Willem's singsong nasal voice, which would've been grating and irritating in any other reader, quite charmed them.

Please put me down for Wil'm Zengler. If there's a list for him, please put my name on it. Thank you!

Her own daddy had been damned good-looking it was said. *Like some movie star of the old days—Alan Ladd?*

No memory of her daddy. Not *damned good-looking*—not anything. Just—no memory.

Vanished when she was just five. That was the story.

No pictures, either. Not a photo surviving.

Snapshots of her mother, scattered among relatives. Only vaguely can she recall.

Doesn't trust good-looking men. The face is a mask, they look at you from behind it. Even older men, if they are smooth-shaven, handsome. Any man with carefully brushed hair. Hint of hair oil, she feels a twinge of nausea. Acrid smell of cigarette smoke, more nausea. Sweetish smell of whiskey on a breath, she begins to breathe quickly, like an asthma attack, can cause a black-out, falling in a dead faint like a puppet whose strings have been cut.

No oil on Willem Zengler's very short hair. No whiskey on his breath—ever!

What is Willem's smell? Soap, toothpaste. Cheerios. When he's been exercising, excited, a frank smell of sweat.

How he'd sweated on their wedding night. Slick-slippery smooth skin of his back, ripple of muscles. Scattering of pimples on the broad, smooth back she'd discovered by chance, miniature constellations beneath her fingertips she doubted Willem himself knew anything about.

A man's naked body. She has not (yet) looked upon it. Nor has Willem (yet) looked upon his bride's naked body, though they have now spent an entire night together in the same bed.

In the Reformed Methodist Church to which Willem's family belongs not even soda pop is allowed. No tobacco, no alcohol (even "lite" beer), chewing gum, junk food, artificial sweeeners. Forbidden things you wouldn't think could have meaning to anyone.

Like believing that God is watching. God is watching what you *eat* or hears you mutter *hell, damn, goddamn.*

God is watching, judging. God will determine that nothing more terrible will happen to you than you can bear.

That is what Christians believe. That seems to be what Willem and his family believe.

Of course, Abby Hayman is a good girl. Abby never mutters "swear" words aloud.

Skele-ton. Skele-tons.

Here is the mistake: to have given into happiness. She will be punished now.

Did you think you could forget us?

Like that sharp, tremulous sensation between her legs, at the fork of her body, when Willem (gently, insistently) touched her there, their wedding night, she'd begun to shudder, to hold herself very still, like a bow that is bent farther, and farther, almost to breaking . . .

But it is a mistake to give in. You cannot begin to fathom what it is like if you give in.

Such sharp, raw, pulsing pleasure, she had never felt it before in her life. Seeming to spring from her young husband's gently cupped hand, and his mouth sucking wetly on her mouth.

You don't deserve such pleasure. Such happiness. So searing, a bright light blinding her dazed eyes.

No one has told her, for there is no one to tell her. But she knows: she does not deserve the happiness of marriage, and of love. There is something special about her, something damned and accursed. In the tall grasses the skulls had regarded her with a mocking sort of calm.

Did you think we could forget you?

In the dream of the previous morning, before she'd become Mrs. Willem Zengler, believing that her life, in all other ways damned, might in this way be saved, the piteous fact is, she'd had no awareness of the presence of love in her life. No memory of a young man, no memory of his name.

In the dream that awaits her, when she dares to shut her eyes, it is another time, a time before love. The time of her truest self, in which Willem does not exist.

No! That is a lie. She is married. Her husband does exist . . .

Miss? You okay?

Tears gather in her eyes. Tears of joy, wonder. That she is safely married. That she is safely loved. Protected. Staring at the narrow silver band around her finger, a Celtic design. Not an expensive ring and (maybe) not entirely silver, but (she thinks) very beautiful.

Her husband wears a matching band. Jewelry store in the shopping center advertising SALE 50% OFF. At this moment her husband is approximately six miles away at the sprawling north campus of the state university.

Why are you lying! You have no husband.

You have dreamed it all. You are evil, sick. Insane.

No decent man would marry you.

Married! A single day.

Brushing at her eyes with her fingertips. Surreptitiously. So ashamed!—crying in a public place, nowhere to hide. Rubbing her wrist, circling her right wrist with her fingers.

Yes we saw her. We'd been noticing her. Not that she was acting really weird but just, like she was talking to herself, or someone was talking to her, all inward. So actually you couldn't notice— much. But she was such a pretty girl, you couldn't miss her.

Some kind of old-fashioned look about her. Not like girls today—high school girls dressing like sluts—but of some other time, the coat she was wearing had a belt, little knitted wool cap on her head, and her hair not straggling straight over her shoulders like most girls, but shorter and kind of neat, wavy. And she's wearing a skirt, actual stockings, and "ballerina" flats the way office girls used to dress. No makeup, it looked like—maybe just lipstick.

There was something strange about her— how she kept rubbing her wrist. Like there was something there, on her wrist, but I couldn't see anything, not even a wristwatch.

Like she was sleepwalking—asleep with her eyes open. Little smile on her lips, until she started crying.

Asked her was she okay but she didn't hear . . .

Suddenly, must get off the bus. Can't breathe. Pulls the cord. Hurry!

On her feet, at the rear door. Calls out to the driver in a voice like a scared child's. *Let me out here, please—here!* The driver scowls at her in the rearview mirror. *Take it easy, miss. Stop's the next block.*

Not her stop (yet) but must get off the bus right now. Whatever is going to happen to her is approaching. Closer!

Not even sure where she is. Two other passengers disembarking when she does, watching her.

Poor girl was breathing hard—like panting. Like she'd been running hard, panting like a dog or a horse. Her face was dead white. Looked like she'd scream if anyone touched her.

Vaguely she is aware, this isn't her stop. Not sure where she is. Can't read the street signs (something wrong with her eyes, as it is sometimes when you try to "read" in a dream) but guesses that this is not—yet—Raritan Avenue. Sudden panic about being late. Willem chides her, often she is late. Comes to look for her and finds her staring at a clock—just staring. As the red second hand moves. Hypnotized by the circular movement of the red second hand. Must escape, must run for her life but—can't move her legs. Traffic noises in her ears. Sees, or thinks she sees, a green light. Then it changes to a red light. Not yellow. She has not seen yellow. Quickly stepping from the curb, blindly into traffic, runs in front of the very bus from which she'd just disembarked, and at once she is struck by the vehicle as it heaves into motion. Knocked off her feet, tossed like a rag doll, her head strikes against the pavement.

Jesus! She just stepped in front of me. Wasn't looking. Head down. Before, on the curb, it looked like she was thinking—making a decision. Then she just steps in front of the bus. Lucky for her I was just pulling out, not going fast. Could've run right over her, crushing her skull or her spine, she'd have died in an instant.

First time in the eleven years I've been driving this bus, this route. Never anything like this before.

And a damned pretty girl. What was she thinking!

"He Vows
He Will Never Leave Her"

He vows he will never leave her.

Even when he must leave her bedside at the hospital, or when she is taken away for tests and for surgery to reduce the pressure of blood on her brain, he will remain as (physically) close to her as he can.

In a hospital corridor, on the other side of swinging doors—NO ADMITTANCE EXCEPT HOSPITAL STAFF.

On the nighttime hospital grounds, in a sleeping bag. Behind a trio of Dumpsters where no one will think to look.

First visitor to enter the hospital when doors open at 6:30 a.m.

Last visitor to leave the ICU, 11:30 p.m.

When she is moved from Intensive Care to a room in the general hospital, as her husband, he will be allowed to remain with her overnight.

In the meantime he remains with her in Intensive Care. Takes as few breaks as possible, on the run. Fearful that she might open her eyes, search for him, call his name, and he won't be there . . .

At her side as she lies unmoving (except for shallow, rapid breathing through a plastic device

33

positioned at her nostrils) in the high hospital bed. Gripping her hand in his.

Convinced that, though her fingers are cold, limp, unresponsive, she can feel his fingers gripping hers. Though her (grotesquely blackened and swollen) eyes are (seemingly) shut, she can "see" dimly, she can recognize him—somewhere inside her brain, where her spirit dwells.

Abby darling, I am here. I will never leave you.
You will be awake, soon—I will be waiting.
I am your husband, I love you.
Do you hear me? I think you do . . .
Squeeze my fingers if you hear me? Abby?

He does think about it. He is tormented, thinking about it.

Was it accidental, was it *deliberate?*

No one will know. No one can know. Unless Abby can recall when she wakes up.

If she wakes up.

And even then, how reliable would Abby's recollection be after the trauma of a brain fracture . . .

Willem slides from the bedside chair, on his knees on the floor. There is consolation in the unyielding hardness of the floor. Pressing his forehead against the metal bedstead. Praying to Jesus, and praying to God.

He knows such prayer is embarrassing to others. Even others who believe in prayer. In the ICU waiting room, much of the day, there are often members of the Zengler family on their knees, praying for Willem's young wife, whom they scarcely know. Tears streaking the cheeks of some, and not just the women and girls. *Our Father who art in heaven, have mercy on our beloved Abby.*

Jesus is Willem's friend. Almost, Willem can see Jesus in a corner of the room.

God is more distant. Willem has never been at ease with God. If Jesus is his friend and also his brother, God is their father.

Jesus, thank you for Abby's life.

Each breath Abby breathes, thank you Jesus.

For the breath of Abby's life when she was born, thank you God.

If there should come to be a choice, God—take my life and let Abby live.

"First Sight"

He didn't believe in anything so superficial, silly—love at first sight.

Still, seeing Abby for the first time—not that he knew her name: he did not—he'd felt an overwhelming sensation of certainty. *That is the girl I will marry.*

He'd known better than to stare at her. He had business of his own. He'd arrived at the Rehabilitation Center for a two-hour reading session with an elderly blind woman who wanted Willem to read to her from a book titled *Constitutional Law: Casebook for Law Students*; her grandson was taking a course in the subject in law school, and she wanted to be able to "argue intelligently" with him.

And there was the pretty girl with a pale, freckled face and the calmest demeanor, one of the younger rehab staff, in a crisply ironed white blouse, a narrow powder-gray skirt, transparent stockings, and the soft-leather black shoes of a dancer, politely listening to the bitter complaints of a man with a puckered face and pits for eyes. The blind man's countenance was as terrible to behold as the countenance of an Old Testament prophet, but the pretty girl with the freckled face did not flinch, nor even try to stem the blind man's anger. With the wisdom of a much older person, she simply let him rant until he was finished, with an expression of peeved satisfaction.

Willem overheard the girl assure the blind man that she would pass on to her supervisor every-thing he'd said. Willem felt a shiver, hearing her soft-rippling, comforting voice, not at all strident or shrill, as girls' and women's voices sometimes were, especially in stressful situations.

He saw that her nails were manicured, filed short, with a transparent glisten. The Reformed Methodist Church did not approve of those long, clawlike bright-polished nails so favored by girls and women, like bright red lipstick and mauve eyelids, that both excited and repelled Willem and his friends.

He saw that there was no ring on her left hand. In fact, no ring on any of her fingers.

He saw that she was kind, patient, sympathetic with an irascible individual whom another might shun. He saw that she was *good*.

He thought—*Yes! She is the one.*

His first conversation with Abby came the following week, after the Rehab Center closed at five p.m. Willem had arranged to be waiting behind the County Services building at the likely door the rehab staff would use, and indeed, there Abby appeared at 5:20, alone. And there Willem Zengler was, sitting on a ledge, his head bent over a book on his lap; he seemed to know that Abby might pause to look at him, recognizing him, for of course they'd been aware of each other at the center. At that moment Willem glanced up, smiled at her as if (mildly, pleasantly) surprised to see her, waved as if (already) they were friends.

"Hi, there!"

"Hi . . ."

Abby had to know Willem's name from the volunteer readers' list, but Willem introduced himself anyway. Abby, explaining that her name was Gabriella, introduced herself as "Abby—that's what people call me."

Several months later, when they became engaged and it was inevitable that Willem would see her birth certificate, Abby confessed to him that her birth-name wasn't Gabriella after all but Miriam Frances—a name she'd always disliked, a harsh-sounding name, a dull, old-lady name, not *her*.

"But your last name is Hayman?"—Willem had to ask, though in a lighthearted way.

"Yes, my last name is Hayman. I wouldn't lie about *that*."

So softly Abby spoke, Willem could scarcely hear her words. She seemed to be stricken with emotion. Not guilt? Shame? For something so trivial?

"I wouldn't call it a lie, honey," Willem said. "People like to name themselves, sometimes.

Lots of people have nicknames. For sure, 'Miriam Frances' isn't *you*."

"Do you think that Abby is more like me?"

"Yes."

"And—Gabriella?"

The most beautiful name he'd ever heard, Willem said extravagantly. But it was a little too special, too exotic, for an everyday name, so it was sensible to call her Abby.

"Thank you!" she said. "I love you."

"I love *you*."

But the tiny pucker remained between Abby's eyes and was slow to fade.

Next time they saw each other, Abby brought up the subject of her name—which in fact Willem had more or less forgotten—saying that she was embarrassed, but she was grateful. She'd expected him to be disgusted with her for making up a pretty name for herself.

"I guess I want to be Abby to some people, mostly my age, who I hope will—like me . . ."

You'd have thought this was a confession to a serious crime! Willem laughed at her and kissed her. He'd have said that he didn't give a damn what her name was, why should he?

It was not uncommon for Willem to use such mild profanities as *damn, hell*—though he would never utter *goddamn*.

Never such a colorful profanity as *goddamn it to hell*.

"What are you called back in Chautauqua Falls?" Willem meant this to be an affable question, for he meant to humor her.

"W-where?"

Abby's expression was blank. A dismaying thought came to Willem—*She has been lying.*

But no, not possible. Not this sweet, guileless girl!

"Chautauqua Falls. Didn't you say that was where you're from? Where you lived with your Aunt Traci . . ."

Abby seemed disoriented, confused. Then, quickly:

"I—I—I was called—I'm not sure . . . It was so long ago . . . I mean, no one ever called me Miriam—you wouldn't call a child Miriam. Maybe it was *Mir*. Meer—Aunt Traci might have called me . . . And before that, my mother called me—I guess—some kind of silly baby name . . ."

"What did people call you in high school? What was your name there?"

"Well, I guess—Abby."

"Abby? But I thought . . ."

"Aunt Traci started all that. I remember now. Abby—Gabriella. *She* thought of it, because we both hated Miriam Frances."

Willem saw that his fiancée was becoming anxious. Good to change the subject, he thought, and never bring it up again.

"Comatose"

It is a place in which time is suspended. Day, nighttime pass in the distance like bloated storm clouds.

Twenty-four hours. Forty-eight hours. Now seventy-two hours—and beyond. Like Sleeping Beauty, the patient lies suspended, neither fully alive nor dead, though breathing on her own, pure oxygen in shallow surges barely visible to the attentive eye.

Sleeping Beauty, who was awakened by a kiss!—Willem is surprised to recall, for fairy tales meant and mean nothing to him.

Though he does lean over the comatose girl to kiss—very lightly—as light as the brush of a butterfly's wing—her swollen and bruised lips.

Not so pretty now, the young wife. Grotesquely lacerated face, blackened eyes, bandages swathing her head. Looking very young, a battered child of indeterminate sex. The girl whom Willem's parents had been determined to love if Willem loved her. If Willem seriously, sincerely loved her.

"Can Abby hear me, Doctor? When I talk to her?"

"Possibly, yes. That is—possible."

The neurologist means to be kind, Willem can

41

see. Adding that whatever his wife might hear in her comatose state, she would probably not remember when she wakes up. As she will probably not remember the accident.

Accident? Willem is grateful to hear this word. It seems to be the consensus—Abby got off the bus, appeared to be confused or distracted, stepped in front of the bus as it pulled from the curb *accidentally,* not deliberately.

"If your wife can hear your voice, it will be very beneficial to her. And if not, nothing is lost."

Willem's heart leaps at the sound of this. *Nothing is lost.*

"Sin"

If you can hear me, Abby? Give a sign.

If you love me, Abby? Give a sign.

No longer measured in hours, but in days. Beyond seventy-two hours, a vast, terrifying expanse stretching to the horizon like the Sahara desert, and Willem is barely capable of acknowledging—*four days? five?*

Soon, unimaginably—*one week.*

His (tireless) hand gripping hers. His fingers (gently) squeezing hers.

Seeing how large his hand is, how her small hand is encased within it.

It continues to amaze him that this young woman is his wife. Mrs. Willem Zengler.

Of course (Willem concedes), they are not yet what you'd call—fully—*man and wife.*

Not, as the Bible says, *one flesh.*

Their wedding night, they'd been giddy, silly, excited, nervous, anxious, shy of each other. Willem, tremulous with love for his bride and with desire, had been fearful of Abby seeing his body too bluntly, in too bright a light—for the first time, for a virgin, that part of him, groin, genitals, erect, engorged penis might be a shock, repugnant.

Glimpsed in a full-length mirror, he's a shock sometimes to himself.

That part of him—since puberty, alarming in its autonomy and total lack of shame, as promiscuous in its appetite as a ravenous bear marauding a campsite.

Other guys, high school shower room, glancing (uneasily) in Willem Zengler's direction. Wanting/not wanting to see. Envy, awe. Glancing quickly away. He'd always been tall, muscled, developed for his age. Took his size for granted. Couldn't imagine being a *little guy*. How the world would look to you from a short height.

Willem isn't a vain young man, despite his good looks, build. Or rather, Willem's masculine vanity envelopes his entire being, and so he is blind to it.

Sex outside marriage: sin. The Church is clear about that. Jesus (maybe) is clear about that. *Lust* is the only sin, Willem thinks, to which he might be tempted.

The Church teaches: sex is for procreation, purely. Anything other than procreation is lust, and lust is forbidden.

Well, alcohol is forbidden, too. Yet Willem has (occasionally, not often) drunk beer with (non-Church) friends, without his family knowing and without serious consequences.

He'd liked the taste of beer, to a degree. Wondering if the fact that it was forbidden made it taste better.

Secretly, without anyone in his family knowing, Willem purchased a (small) bottle of champagne for their wedding night.

Not French champagne, which was much too expensive. A local, New York State champagne at half the price of the French.

"Just this once won't hurt us," Willem told Abby.

Abby giggled, shivered. So skittish, Willem could see the tiny pale hairs on her bare arm lift when he brushed against her. And her breath was coming as quick and shallow as the breath of a wild creature that has found itself in some sort of captivity.

Had Abby ever drunk anything alcoholic?— Willem supposed not.

"Just a half glass for each of us. I promise it will be okay, Abby."

Still, Abby was looking uncertain. Though she wasn't (yet) baptized in the Reformed Methodist Church, she seemed to have promised Willem's parents that she would join the church soon after the wedding.

After a struggle Willem managed to open the champagne bottle. Pouring a few inches of the enchanting, fizzing liquid into their glasses, which were only ordinary glasses but adequate to their purpose.

Excited, elated, in a state of near euphoria underlaid with dread, Willem touched his glass against Abby's, and drank. In imitation of him, Abby took an experimental sip.

"Oh! It's so—*strong* . . ."

Through much of the wedding day Willem had been unusually quiet, but now, alone with his bride in the sparely furnished one-bedroom apartment they'd rented within walking distance of the Raritan Avenue bus line, he had much to tell her.

Explaining to her his "policy" on names.

In his family, people didn't believe in shortened names—nicknames. Willem was named for a great-grandfather who'd died at almost the very hour Willem had been born. No one believed in reincarnation, a pagan superstition, but still, you had to wonder. God had some intention.

Other names in the family were taken from the Bible—Jeremiah, Samson, Ezekiel.

That's how they will name their children, Willem said. They will each participate, making a list of names from the Bible.

Abby giggled, shocked. Blushing.

Was she agreeing to something she will regret? The champagne makes everything feel easy. Like lifting your hand to brush away coarse cobwebs and the webs disintegrate in your hand.

Willem wasn't sure how he felt about sin— that is, the idea of it. That people committed acts designated as *sins,* thus were sinners. Except for deliberate acts of evil that hurt others, Willem thought that sin was mistaken behavior, making

46

a wrong decision based upon faulty reasoning. Jesus was a guide to avoiding such mistakes, but Jesus did not believe in punishment.

Jesus believes in love, not hate. Jesus forgives, not condemns.

Jesus teaches us to avoid sin—not because it is sinful, but because it is a mistake.

"But what about Hell?" Abby asked doubtfully.

"The hell with Hell!" The champagne was delicious and had gone instantly to Willem's head.

"Don't you believe in Hell, Willem?—I guess I do." Abby spoke wistfully.

Willem laughed again, and kissed her, and poked his champagne tongue into her startled little mouth, and said, "Let's forget Hell for tonight, Abby. It's our honeymoon."

So, each had a half a glass of champagne. And then another. Laughing, breathless in bed.

Their bed. First time.

Not long after, each had fallen asleep. Still, a light was burning in the bedroom and they were not entirely unclothed.

Willem woke himself with a snort. Had he been asleep? Snoring? At such a time?

Abby was sleeping, as calm as a baby. Though there was a tiny pucker between her eyes. She'd purchased a new nightgown, of some soft-satiny cerise color, with an oddly high collar, long sleeves. Willem would have liked to caress her through the nightgown, but he did not. He would have liked to kiss her lips lightly, to wake her, but he did not. Stealthily he crept into the bathroom, decided not to flush the toilet and (possibly) wake his sleeping wife—making a mental note to rise early, to return to the bathroom to flush the toilet before Abby used it—and returned breathless, switching off the light, climbing into bed as quietly as possible, and gathering Abby into his arms without waking her.

So happy! Joy swept through his being. He knew himself transported, transformed. His parents' misgivings about the marriage, and about his dear bride, seemed to him now totally groundless.

Therefore a man shall leave his father and his mother and hold fast to his wife, and they shall become one flesh.

He slept heavily until dawn. Waking excited and aroused, and in his nostrils the commingled sweet smells of champagne, bedclothes, Abby's hair and skin.

But Abby was whimpering in her sleep. Squirming, agitated.

What was she saying? Should he wake her?

Was it eavesdropping, to listen to another person speaking in her sleep?

But he couldn't decipher what she was saying. Clearly she was upset, frightened. Her breath came quick and short, like panting. She was beginning to thrash about. It was distressing to the young husband to realize that his wife was upset by a dream, and to not know what it was.

"Abby, darling? Wake up, you're having a nightmare . . ."

With difficulty Abby woke, like one pushing her way to the surface of water with agitated motions of her limbs. Her eyes opened, shocked and confused. For a moment she seemed not to recognize Willem who was leaning over her on an elbow.

"Abby? Honey? It was just a dream . . ."

In that instant, as she stared at him, Willem felt a twinge of fear—that she would strike out at him, scream at him.

What had Abby been seeing in the depths of sleep? A sort of convulsive paralysis had overcome her. Willem felt as if he were wrestling with something, another being, a creature, a thing that had hold of her and did not want to relinquish her.

Her eyes were widened, dilated. Her skin was white, clammy-cold. She was shivering, her teeth chattering with cold.

Willem wondered if he should ask her what she'd been dreaming—but maybe it was better for her to forget.

Even bad dreams are just vapor. He would kiss her and embrace her, and comfort her, and . . .

She pushed away from him, panicked. She murmured an apology—*"Sorry! Sorry."* Fled into the bathroom.

Oh, damn! He'd meant to hurry into the bathroom before her and flush the toilet. He'd totally forgotten.

In their bed Willem lay staring at the ceiling. Listening to the drumming of the shower. Telling himself it was natural, it was normal, his (virginal) young wife was frightened of him. Not *him,* but the intimacy of their bodies in bed.

Neither was prepared. Especially, he supposed, Abby was not prepared. He'd witnessed her wincing if she heard someone utter profanities, a flush came into her face, a look of misery, as if she wished badly to be elsewhere.

As her husband, he would protect her. That was his mission. He would never force her to do anything she did not feel comfortable doing, he'd worked that out beforehand. He felt some small measure of relief that the ordeal of making love with his skittish virginal wife for the first time had been postponed.

Willem's first time, too. But he was not so worried about himself.

Both were scheduled to leave the apartment at about the same time that morning. Neither had wished to ask for time off that day—Abby at the Rehabilitation Center, Willem at the university. As Abby prepared to leave, she became less agitated, calmer; she regained something of her sense of humor and did not stiffen when Willem kissed her as she buttoned her coat, adjusted a little lavender knitted cap on her head. Though it was early April, the air was still wintry, gusty. Only a few days earlier, the last stubborn remnants of rotted-looking snow had melted in places most hidden from the sun.

Here was an oddity: somewhere in the apartment, it seemed, Abby had found a length of twine, about ten inches long, and had wound it several times around her right wrist, tightly. This she'd done in the bathroom, Willem assumed. "What's that?" he asked, and Abby said, "Nothing. It's— nothing," as if for the moment she'd forgotten about the twine, and had no idea what it was, except that it was embarrassing to her that Willem saw it.

Quickly she tugged it off and turned away. Willem saw that her slender wrist was circled with a rashlike red mark.

Should he offer to kiss her wrist, make it well? Better not.

He was determined not to be hurt. The way Abby had seemed to panic, push out of his arms, and hide in the bathroom . . . How mortified he would be if his brothers or (male) cousins knew! They'd been joking about Willem before the wedding, his (presumed) inexperience. (And what "experience" did they have? Willem was skeptical.)

He understood that the newlywed wife was relieved to be leaving the apartment and the husband, calmed by the prospect of being alone again, if even for a few hours. Oh, he understood! Every girl he knew well—girls in his family, girls from church—was shy about her body, excessively self-conscious about her appearance. The prettier and more feminine the girl, the more self-conscious. He could see that Abby was grateful that he, Willem, was as understanding as he was, for all his inexperience. Not trying to touch her, let alone restrain her, or reason or argue with her; not expressing anger, disappointment as (surely) another man might have done in his place.

Wounded male vanity. Sex vanity. Willem was superior to that.

"It will be different tonight, Abby," he said. "I promise."

Not clear what he meant, but he smiled bravely and kissed his wife another time, and Abby kissed him in return, not quite on the lips but warmly, sincerely, before hurrying away on the stairs to catch the Raritan Avenue bus.

Later, Willem would discover the twine discarded in a wastebasket.

In the late morning the call came for him at the university—*Is this William Zengler? Next-of-kin of Abby Zengler? I am so sorry to tell you, Mr. Zengler, your wife was struck by a bus downtown, this morning, and has been taken to the ER at the Hammond Medical Clinic.*

Stalking

He didn't think so. No.

Since he was her fiancé, how could he be her stalker?

He loved her, and he was reasonably sure that she loved him. Hardly the circumstances that defined *stalking*.

Except: he was curious about her. Not just his parents, sisters, and brothers inquiring about her, virtually all the relatives, even the neighbors and friends—*Who is this girl Abby? Who are her people?* Willem himself wanted to know all that he could know about her without (this was essential) her being aware.

He could not risk it, that Abby would think he didn't trust her. For in fact he trusted her, absolutely. He knew she trusted him, for she asked him virtually no questions about his life, his family, his background—"Whoever you are, who's Willem, that's all I care about. Not even your last name. That's the person I love—*you*."

So fiercely Abby spoke, with such childlike trust in him, Willem felt a stab of guilt. For he did feel curiosity about her, apart from his family's queries, which w re annoying to him and which he resented.

She'd told him about naming herself—

Abby—out of a dislike for her birth name. She told him that she was from "west of here"—"near the Pennsylvania border"—"south of Erie." Or, she'd once lived there but had moved as a young child, living with relatives in the Chautauqua area.

Her parents had died when Abby was a young child, Willem believed. It wasn't clear to him whether they'd died at the same time, in an automobile accident perhaps, or at different times. Or maybe one of them had died and the other was simply out of her life.

"Sounds like you were a kind of orphan."

"No! I *was not* an orphan."

Willem had meant to be sympathetic, but Abby seemed hurt. He'd squeezed her hand to make amends.

Abby explained, "I never was an orphan. I was always with relatives. I lived with my aunt Traci for a long time, in Chautauqua Falls. I told you about her. I loved—*love*—my aunt Traci . . ."

Though later, after they were engaged and Willem suggested driving to Chautauqua Falls to meet Abby's aunt, Abby said evasively that it wasn't a good time for a visit at the moment. Her aunt Traci was in the midst of the school term (she was a middle school teacher) and was having "health problems." Still later, Aunt Traci was selling her house and moving into another house, and there were many "legal complications."

Eventually the mysterious Aunt Traci would be

unable to attend Abby's wedding for "personal reasons"—so Abby was informed only a day or two before the wedding.

"That's too bad, Abby. I hope you're not too disappointed . . ."

"Oh, no! I am never disappointed. Whatever happens, or doesn't happen, was never meant to be anything but the way it turned out, except you don't know it ahead of time. Then, looking back, you can see it all makes sense. You were silly to expect anything different just because it might be something flattering to you."

"Really? Silly?"—Willem had to smile at Abby's logic. He had not a clue what she was talking about, but he rarely contradicted her, as he might have contradicted a man, for instance. You expected men to make sense, but a pretty girl, looking like a schoolgirl, especially one so sweet as Abby—who adored him, and who often became nervous or uneasy when he questioned her—was different.

Several times he'd sighted Abby, or someone who closely resembled her, in the vicinity of the County Services building as he was arriving at the Rehabilitation Center for the Blind, or departing. Once, it was certainly Abby walking beside a man (in a suit) in a corridor of the building, too far away for Willem to attract her attention and wave. In the city center of Hammond, amid a rectangle of municipal buildings linked by a small green square, office workers often ate their lunch outside in good weather, and once, Willem sighted Abby on a bench with another girl, or woman, older than Abby, who was not eating lunch as Abby was, but smoking a cigarette and wagging a crossed leg. Abby appeared to be silent, listening as the woman spoke earnestly to her, making a stabbing gesture with her lighted cigarette to emphasize her words.

Willem observed them from across the square. He would not have thought he was spying on his fiancée, it was just that he loved her so much.

It was like gazing at a beautiful butterfly or a bird. Hummingbird?

Who was the woman and what was she saying to Abby in that forceful, annoying way? Willem was fascinated.

There seemed to be a family resemblance between them, Willem thought. Though Abby was very beautiful, and the other, older woman was not attractive at all.

Where Abby was dressed for the office in secretarial attire, as she might have called it— skirt, blouse, stockings, good flat-heeled shoes— her companion wore slacks, a T-shirt, slovenly sandals, and was obviously not an office worker. The woman's short-cropped hair was bleached ash-blond, her face looked as if it had been scrubbed shiny-hard, with a scattering of freckles like dirty raindrops.

Offensive to Willem, how this woman wagged her leg. (Did Abby not notice?) How this woman smoked a cigarette in a public place, jabbing with the cigarette and scattering ashes, exhaling smoke from mouth, nostrils. (Did Abby not notice? Why was Abby so tolerant of this crude, coarse, unfeminine behavior?)

Of course, Willem understood that women and girls no longer had to present themselves as "feminine" to the male gaze. Older Zengler relatives objected to women wearing shorts and jeans in public places and were vehement in never voting for any woman candidate for office, but Willem didn't identify with these.

It was just that a man naturally *preferred* a feminine woman or girl. A man could hardly help preferring a pretty face, a soft voice, a happy-seeming smile . . .

Willem deliberated whether to approach Abby on the park bench, to say hello. It was entirely appropriate that he'd seen her in this public place, happened to see her, though there was no particular reason for him to have turned up at County Services that day, for it wasn't the Christian Youth volunteer day.

He wouldn't lie to Abby if she questioned him. But it wasn't like her to be suspicious of others' motives.

Finally, Willem came forward. Abby greeted him a bit distractedly, for indeed she didn't expect to see him; she introduced him to her companion—Noreen—who, as it turned out, was no one of any consequence, not (evidently) a friend or a relative.

(Why was Noreen talking so intently to Abby? And why was Abby listening so intently? Willem never learned.)

Soon afterward, Willem's mother asked him if he'd ever met any relative of his fiancée's, and Willem heard himself saying yes, he had.

To confound his mother, *yes*.

"I met one of Abby's cousins. A woman named Noreen."

"Really! Does she live around here?"

"Chautauqua Falls."

"And—what does she do?"

"What does she *do?* I think she teaches middle school."

"Well—when are we going to meet Abby's relatives?"

"At the wedding. Maybe."

"At the wedding. Who will be coming?"

Willem stood silent, stubborn. Being interrogated by his parents had been part of his life since childhood, and he was resenting it now that he was no longer a child.

"You know what Abby is like, Mom. Who her family is, what's her background—none of that is relevant."

"No, that isn't true, Willem," his mother protested. "When two young people marry, their families marry too . . ."

Willem disliked those smug, exasperating Christians who quoted Bible verses to support their opinions, but here he was, in a quiet voice, confounding his mother further with the verse that had lately become his favorite—"'Therefore a man shall leave his father and his mother . . . '" ending with the most thrilling and audacious words a young man might utter to a startled mother—"'one flesh.'"

Awake

"Abby! My God."

Suddenly it happens. After nine days Abby opens her eyes, regains what is called consciousness—dazed, confused, scarcely able to speak, but at least now awake and (seemingly) herself again.

In her (bloodshot, blackened) eyes, Willem can see *her*. The eyes are alert, focused, alive.

And when Willem squeezes her hand, Abby squeezes back.

I love you.

Willem is giddy, ecstatic. He shouts for joy. He laughs, he cries. He cannot believe how lucky they are, that God has had mercy on them. So many who suffer, Willem tells anyone who will listen—his family, the medical staff, visitors to other patients in ICU—are not blessed by God, but abandoned.

A strange word for the elated young husband to utter—*abandoned*.

When they are alone together, Willem tells Abby he'd like to bring a bottle of champagne to the room, to celebrate their good fortune, as soon as Abby is strong enough to drink champagne. But Abby, squinting and blinking, trying to smile, doesn't seem to comprehend his jubilant words.

Her eyes dart about, alert and alarmed, the pupils dilated. Her swollen lips move; she can manage just a whisper.

Am I . . . alive? What is this place?

"Concussion" means that your brain was jolted against the interior of the brain casing of your skull, causing you to lose consciousness. We are not sure how long—at least several minutes. The liquid that protects the brain was so agitated when you were hit by the bus, and your head struck the pavement, the brain was not protected as it usually is.

But the good news is: you are healing.

Abby is moved from Intensive Care to a less restricted hospital unit called Telemetry. Her vital signs—heartbeat, blood pressure, oxygen intake—are still monitored by beeping machines, but there is little doubt that the patient will pull through. Flowers arrive, even balloons, and soft, stuffed animals. Who has sent these? The Zenglers? Abby's coworkers? Very likely, the excited young husband has brought the festive gifts to the room himself.

After nine days in a comatose state, nine days of being fed intravenously, Abby has lost a good deal of weight. When she'd been brought into the ER, her weight was one hundred and three pounds; now it has dropped to eighty-six. She is five feet three inches tall.

She must continue to breathe pure oxygen through the plastic device positioned at her nostrils. She will remain on an IV drip but will be fed substantial food gradually. For the time being she is being sustained by a bland, odorless mush called mechanical soft.

When will Abby be well enough to be discharged from the hospital? Willem is eager to know. Though it is obvious that she will have to spend time, perhaps weeks, in a rehabilitation clinic, where she will relearn the use of muscles that have become atrophied, feats of motor coordination taken for granted by the healthy.

What has happened to me? Why am I here?

Willem isn't sure what Abby is trying to ask him, although he is more capable of understanding her hoarse, scraping whispers than anyone else.

I will be late for work. They will wonder where I am, at work . . .

Abby is agitated, confused. Willem is told to let her sleep, not to exhaust her by being so frequently at her bedside. But he so badly wants her to be well again, to come home with him, where a wife belongs.

He has been granted a leave of absence from the university. He has explained his situation, and he will not be penalized for missing classes. He plans to return for the summer session, for by then Abby should be fully recovered.

He too has lost weight, and he seems changed

to his troubled family. No longer so youthful and boyish, so *good.*

He has ceased shaving. Coarse whiskers spring from his jaws. His hair, usually kept trimmed, has begun to curl and tangle over his collar. If he'd been stoic on Abby's behalf when she was first hospitalized, now he is becoming more emotional, less predictable in his moods.

It is particularly distressing to Willem that Abby can't seem to remain awake and alert for very long. After half an hour, forty minutes—her eyelids begin to droop. The effort of consciousness seems too great for her to maintain, and the strain of witnessing this effort is exhausting to him as well.

His parents beg him to come home with them for the night. Sleep in his old room. Someone will stay with Abby until visiting hours are over, and in the morning Willem can return.

But Willem is adamant: no.

"Abby needs me *here.*"

Watching her sleep. A tense, twitchy sleep. Her eyelids flutter. The eyeballs within seem to be writhing, jerking in their sockets.

She tries to speak in her sleep. Her mouth begins to contort. A perfect *O* of horror, but the only sound is of moaning, whimpering.

What is she seeing? Willem wonders.

He will shake her awake, as gently as possible.

But Abby seems never to remember what she has been dreaming about.

Her wrists are so thin. Willem sees with horror that he could snap them between thumb and forefinger in a careless gesture.

Accidental, or deliberate? Still, Willem wonders.

He is waiting for the ideal time to question his wife. He understands that he must not upset her.

Police have investigated the incident and determined that it was an accident. The bus driver has been exonerated. No one is legally culpable. The consensus of witnesses is that the young woman getting off the bus was distracted by something, wasn't watching where she was going, stepped out blindly into traffic.

Happens all the time. What's meant by *accident*.

There is more to it, Willem thinks. *He* will find out.

Newlyweds

"Oh! Is that . . . *me?*"

The first time Abby is allowed to see her reflection in a hand mirror provided by a nurse, she stares in dismay, laughs.

She has learned to laugh again, a harsh, hoarse sound that startles Abby herself. She winces with pain when she smiles, but she smiles.

A battered face, a row of thin, pale scars at her hairline. Will the scars fade in time? Willem assures Abby, yes certainly.

"You can hardly see them now unless you're up close. Unless the light is bright."

A visitor, one of Willem's relatives, suggests "cosmic surgery" if the scars don't fade.

Willem objects: "Abby is beautiful to me, whatever she looks like."

Abby laughs. Her incensed young husband's words are very funny.

Living in a body. *That* is the joke.

But there is good news: after less than a week in Telemetry, Abby is being transferred to the general hospital.

Her vital signs have steadily improved. Her blood work, her X-rays. She is able to eat solid, if soft foods. She can drink through a straw without choking, she is regaining weight. Her mouth is no longer swollen and misshapen. (She doesn't wince and shrink away if her husband tries to kiss her.) The bruises on her face, like wrathful storm clouds, have begun to fade.

The punctured lung is mending slowly. Broken collarbone, broken and sprained ribs—slow to heal. But healing. Abby has learned that her body is a fragile vessel. Never again will she entirely trust a seemingly flat surface beneath her feet not to swerve suddenly and pitch her forward . . .

Told by a nurse to *just lie still, dear. This may pinch.*

In an instant, beneath the covers, the (hateful) catheter is detached from a part of her body Abby has not glimpsed in a long time.

As she has not attempted to use the toilet by herself in what seems like a long time.

Hoping she won't have an embarrassing accident en route, Abby is helped from her bed by a cheerful nurse's aide, makes her way shakily into the bathroom.

Next time, Willem will help her. Willem insists.

"I'm your husband. I can do lots of things for you. You don't always need *them*."

Abby is surprised, her clean-shaven young husband is growing a beard. He is letting his hair grow long, unruly. The Zenglers are not happy with this change in their son, but Abby thinks he looks more like a biblical prophet.

Curtly, Willem has told his parents that he

doesn't care what he looks like. His focus is on Abby, not himself.

Willem continues to pray for her, several times a day. His prayers are as simple and direct as telegrams—*Dear God, make Abby well again. Amen!*

(Abby is too modest to pray on her own behalf. Whatever has happened to her has happened for a reason, and that reason is God's plan.)

Willem sits in a chair near the window in Abby's hospital room, reading a massive biology textbook and making notations with a yellow Magic Marker. Some of his notations are question marks. He'd dropped out of the Introduction to Biology course at the university but has become fascinated by the subject. *Why* did God create pain in the world, for instance? Humankind might be punished for Adam and Eve's sin, but why would animals be made to suffer?

"Having nerves makes us vulnerable to terrible suffering," Willem tells Abby. "It might have been different. No nerves—no pain. God made some kind of decision."

It isn't clear whether Abby follows Willem's speculations. She tries to remain alert when he addresses her but her eyelids often droop.

"Also, you have to wonder why God made certain things—rabies, flesh-eating bacteria, pancreatic cancer that can kill in a few weeks. The more you know about it, there's lots in nature that doesn't make sense."

Willem's family believes that the answers to Willem's questions, as to all questions that matter, are found in the Bible. And any questions that can't be answered by the Bible do not matter.

"God doesn't do something for no reason," Willem says stubbornly. "I really don't believe that."

The Zenglers are not happy that their son has become so interested in biology, as he has in other science courses at the university, but they are hesitant to criticize him, for he isn't so docile or pliant as he'd once been, before becoming a married man. But they are still hopeful that he will become a doctor, the first among the Zengler relatives.

Willem isn't so sure about getting an M.D. There are other ways of bringing good to the world, he says.

"Biology is a way of looking at the world when you subtract God," Willem says. "It doesn't bother me, the way it bothers some people, that God is absent in science. Anything I read, I just add in my head—*This is how God made it.*" Willem laughs, pleased with himself. "I just won't write it on the exam, that's all."

Willem glances over at Abby to see that she has fallen asleep. Slack-mouthed, a glisten of saliva on her chin.

He is suffused with love for her, his dear wife.

Yet, he is suffused with curiosity about her. For

there is much that Abby never tells him, he has begun to realize.

Not that Willem is suspicious. Certainly he is not possessive.

Willem watches his wife sleep, fascinated. Across her face shadows flutter like bats' wings.

What is she *seeing,* and what is she *thinking?*

Sometimes her sleep is peaceful, and sometimes it is not. Willem has insisted that Abby be given minimum doses of sedatives and painkillers—he doesn't want his wife to return home addicted.

It is distressing to him when Abby grimaces and moans in her sleep. Her face becomes contorted, as if she is seeing something terrible, unspeakable. Unable to draw a deep breath to call for help.

Still, Willem is reluctant to wake her. He has been told that sleep is infinitely valuable to the patient. Sleep enhances healing.

Poor Abby! Not so pretty now. Her hair is thin, ravaged; there is a shaved strip at the back of her head. Even her freckles look faded, like old tears.

But Willem, stubborn and defiant Willem, loves her more than ever. He will show his parents and others who'd doubted the wisdom of his marriage: a few scars will not deter him from loving his wife. If Abby had been paralyzed or what is called brain-dead, Willem would not have forsaken her.

Soon after the accident, Willem's mother wept bitterly. *Oh! Willem! What have you done! Married this girl you don't even know, and now what will happen to you? What will happen to us?*

Willem told his mother that he'd married Abby because he loved her. And if he had to spend the rest of his life caring for her, he would do that, because he loved her and because Jesus would give him strength.

Their souls were bound together, Willem told his mother. *One flesh.*

In early May, Abby is encouraged to walk in the hospital corridor. Each day a little farther, and eventually she will circle the floor.

Of course she doesn't walk unassisted. She must make her (halting) way leaning on an aluminum walker, pulling an IV drip beside her on wheels. Left ankle, like concrete, dragging at her. Willem supports her with an arm around her waist.

So thin! Abby's waist is *so thin.*

The medical staff is impressed with the very young Mrs. Zengler, who is trying so hard to recover from her injuries. And with the young Mr. Zengler, so devoted to his wife.

Abby's doctors are enthusiastic about her progress. Nurses greet the newlyweds with big smiles. They tell Abby that she is doing so well because she has such a loving husband.

Abby squints at them. Husband? Does she have a husband?

For there is no one beside her. (Is there?)

Her peripheral vision has become blurred. As

she turns her head slowly, objects begin to fade out of sight in the corner of her eye.

Yet someone *is* beside her. A tall young man, close beside her. Arm around her waist, whiskers grazing the sensitive skin of her face.

Oh! Who is *this?*—Abby shivers, laughing.

The young couple are the kind of newlyweds who joke often. It's true that they are Christians, at least Willem identifies strongly as Christian, but not the kind of somber-faced Christians who take themselves too seriously.

Dear God, make Abby well again. Amen!

Willem hovers outside the fMRI room while Abby endures a second test. An fMRI is not an X-ray exactly, Willem has been told. (He fears his wife receiving too much radiation. He fears the point at which medical attention becomes unnatural, contrary to God's intentions.)

Sometimes, alone in a hospital corridor in a part of the hospital unfamiliar to him, Willem wonders if in fact his wife has died. He'd had a wife, and his wife had fled from him, a beautiful girl, face of an angel, he'd failed to keep safe, he'd failed to keep from harm. In revulsion at his body she'd fled from him and had died in a tragic accident out on the street.

Yet somehow the neurologist is telling Willem good news. He wonders how this is possible.

The neurologist is a man of Willem's father's

71

age. It is natural for Willem to respect Dr. Collier, as he would respect any elder. Crushing his hands between his knees as he sits, scarcely daring to breathe, listening to the neurologist reading from a laptop computer screen.

His wife had bled into her brain, Willem is told, and yet—the brain is healing. Her locomotion has been affected, but therapy should help restore her balance and coordination.

The good news is, if all continues to go well, his wife will be discharged to a rehab clinic in approximately a week.

The neurologist shakes Willem's hand. He is shorter than Willem by several inches. Willem is dazed with happiness, not altogether certain that he should believe what he has been told.

Wife? Do I have a wife?—he is about to blurt out, but decides against it.

A clumsy joke, embarrassing to share with a stranger. Not even funny, Willem thinks.

To celebrate the good news, Willem enters Abby's hospital room with a pot of vivid red tulips in his arms and a toy tin whistle between his lips, which he blows just loud enough to rouse her and to make her laugh. He yanks the blinds to the very top of the window—the sky outside is revealed to be a bright, intense blue, like wet paint, that hurts the eyes.

Willem pushes Abby in a wheelchair to the elevator, takes her to the rooftop seven floors above. Here, spring sunshine falls upon their faces, which feel pale, malnourished.

On the hospital rooftop are benches, sun umbrellas, daffodils and tulips in ceramic urns. Several patients in hospital gowns and robes sit lifting their faces to the sun. All are attended by relatives or nurse's aides. But the wind is gusty in spurts, whipping their hair.

Willem asks Abby what she sees. He has rolled the wheelchair to the edge of the building, bumping against an iron railing.

Abby blinks and squints, as if uncertain where she is. The fMRI exam has left her exhausted. Possibly, she is asleep even now. Possibly, she is still in the terrible crashing tunnel from which there was no escape.

They have given Abby tinted glasses to wear, the May sunshine is so bright.

Several times since she has been able to speak coherently Abby has tried to ask Willem about the hospital: Who will pay for it? So many days— nights—in a hospital bed! She has no insurance, no savings. Vaguely Willem has assured her that his family has promised to help. "They will lend us what they can. And other relatives will help us. We will repay them when we can."

Abby considers this. Just when Willem thinks she hasn't heard him, Abby says, with shivery laughter, "It's too late for me to die, I guess. I mean—now. That time would've been in the beginning. If we'd wanted to save money. Or before they brought me here in the ambulance."

Willem laughs, pained. Willem asks if Abby remembers "when you were brought here in the ambulance."

No. Really, she doesn't remember.

"So much of what I say is not true, Willem. I am so ashamed. But—it's like scraping at sand. Beneath the sand there is just more. Sand."

Abby speaks with childlike candor. She is eager to stand on her feet in the open air. Willem helps her, awkwardly. She clutches at him, managing to remain standing.

One small step, and then another. Abby will make her way from the wheelchair to the nearest bench. In one direction are maple trees just coming into leaf, in another direction what appears to be a sea of glistening, broken things but must be, in fact, a parking lot.

Abby stares and stares. Why is the world so dark? she wonders, realizing then that she is wearing tinted glasses with cardboard frames that cut against her ears and nose.

Willem speaks carefully. As if he has rehearsed his words.

"Sometimes you have bad dreams, Abby. This morning, I think you did. What are you dreaming of, do you remember?"

Quickly Abby shakes her head. *No.*

"I think it's something you see. Something

close to your face. Your eyes are moving rapidly from side to side. Behind your closed eyelids. What are you seeing, darling?"

Darling is a somewhat new word between them. Abby thinks, *Darling means coercion.*

Willem continues: "On the morning after we were married, you left our apartment early. You took the Raritan Avenue bus as you always do on your way to work. But why did you get out at the wrong stop?"

Abby appears to be listening. Behind the tinted lenses, her eyes are shut.

"You rang the pull cord, the bus driver said. You were anxious to leave the bus. But you had to wait for the bus to stop. Then you got off the bus and stood on the curb. Try to see the curb, Abby. Try to see the sidewalk. Try to see the bus. Why did you leave the bus before your stop? Was there someone on the bus who threatened you?"

Abby shakes her head, weakly. *No, no. No.*

The wind is gusty, distracting. Abby feels too tired to try to protect her hair from the wind, for this will require lifting her arms. Willem approaches her, his hands at his sides. If she becomes faint suddenly in the breathless wind, if she loses her balance and falls from the bench, he will catch her. Willem is always prepared to catch her.

Abby appears to be thinking. How to answer his question. Is she trying to remember, or is she slipping away from him? The journey in the wheelchair, though it involved no muscular effort on Abby's part, seems to have exhausted her.

"We need to get to that moment, Abby. When you can tell me what you see." Willem speaks gently, reasonably. His heart is beating rapidly, but he is careful to give no sign of his excitement.

"What do you see, Abby? We are not leaving this place until you tell me what you see."

Possibly, Willem hasn't (yet) uttered these words. It is not like Willem to speak in such a way to anyone, let alone his wife.

Abby whimpers like a frightened child. Her ravaged hair is whipping in the wind. The wind is too harsh for May; they have been lured outside and onto the hospital rooftop unwisely.

Thunderclouds have obscured the sun. Suddenly it is as cold as late winter. Abby shivers, shakes her head as if to clear it. She has become dazed, dizzy. She tries to rise from the bench, but her knees buckle.

With a cry Willem catches her before she falls. He pushes the wheelchair to her, helps her into it, secures her legs. He removes his flannel shirt and wraps it around her.

"Darling, I am sorry! Never again."

Willem is stricken with guilt. He has not meant to upset her. In pursuit of the unspeakable secret he believes his young wife harbors, he has pushed too hard.

76

Contrite, Willem will wheel Abby back downstairs to her room. He will kiss her bruised mouth lightly. He will kiss her cold hands. He will help her back into the high, hard bed. While she sinks into the exhausted sleep of oblivion, he will watch jealously over her.

He will not pursue her further; he can't risk exhausting her.

Of course he intends to pursue her further.

Handcuffs

That moment. Just before it happened.

We need to return to that moment.

Trying to tell him—she can't remember.

Trying to plead with him—no . . .

. . .whatever it was she'd seen. Her eyes had seen.

. . .whatever it was in the tall grasses.

Trying to shape the words with her mouth, but her mouth is contorted. Twisted like a Halloween mask. One of those rubber masks so ugly, so disfigured and deformed you hide your eyes from it . . .

Trying to explain to him that it is a mistake for him to love her. For she is not worthy of love.

This is how she is being punished, and her punishment is deserved.

A terrible thing she did. Said. Wanting to utter the words her father wished for her to utter. For she had seen, in his face, desire like a flame. Wanting her to say *yes* to his questions. And so she did.

Yes yes yes yes. She did!

Just a little girl. Five years old. How was it her fault?

But it is. You know it is. *Her fault.*

• • •

Shaheen is not a name she has allowed herself to recall. Not in a long time.

Not in a long time the smell of damp grasses, sun-bleached boulders in the creek bed. In summer, the stream had narrowed to a thin trickling through rocks that glistened and glittered in the sun like the scales of a long, slithering snake.

Not a rattlesnake. She'd seen, once, a thick, fat, frantic rattlesnake hacked to death with an ax. Later, the four-foot rattlesnake skin nailed to the side of a barn to dry in the sun.

Daddy had said in a voice that lifted like a rooster crowing, *Who wants a nice snakeskin belt?*

But it was years later now, after Daddy had gone away. And Mommy had gone away.

Following the (lonely) path along the narrow creek to see where it led. An overgrown path, no one had walked here in a long time.

Her aunt did not want her wandering far from the house. Dense grasses, wild rose, poison ivy. Pastures allowed to grow wild. Rotted planks over the old well. Rotted roofs, a sunken silo. In wet weather the old manure pile in the barnyard stank so you could hardly breathe. In dry weather the barnyard buzzed with horseflies whose stings were as painful as the stings of hornets.

There were no cows, horses, sheep, goats, or

chickens living on the farm any longer. Yet the manure from these creatures remained.

The old Hayman farm—nine acres. No one in the family farmed any longer. Everyone had died or moved away and lived in town.

They'd lived in town—Chautauqua Falls. When she was very little, before she started school. Even then, Daddy had not wanted to live on the farm in Shaheen, though he liked to say it was *my legacy.*

Mommy had always lived in town. Daddy claimed that people in town thought they were better than people who lived in the country, but Mommy always said no, that was not correct. *She* had never thought she was better than anyone else, not ever.

Yeh, you do. Sure.

I do not! Stop saying that.

Well—our little gal is a princess, isn't she? Just like her mommy. Sure she is.

But now she'd become a stray. Like a stray dog, stray cat.

(She'd heard one of the relatives remark of her—*stray.* Maybe he'd been joking, for adults are always joking. But maybe not.)

Since her parents had abandoned her, she'd become a stray. Shuttled from one relative to another. Aunt Traci was the nicest of all, for Aunt Traci would keep her the longest. Aunt Traci was not married and had no children of her own.

It was too bad that Aunt Traci had money problems. Bad luck, she'd loaned money to a (male) friend, and he'd walked out on her. She'd had an accident with her car, walked with a cane, lopsided and angry, claiming that one leg had become shorter than the other. Her eyes were always watering; she blamed chemical fertilizers used by local farmers. Her gums bled easily. Evicted from her place in town, she went to live in the old Hayman farmhouse, taking the stray with her.

Like camping out, she said. Try to make the best of it.

The farmhouse wasn't heated, the roof leaked, windows were cracked or broken, mattresses were infested with roaches, and the walls were infested with mice. Aunt Traci made one (upstairs) room habitable with nylon quilted sleeping bags for herself and for Meer-me, laid upon the floor.

Views from all the windows were beautiful. Uncultivated fields, rolling hills. Dense woods. A glimpse of the unpaved Carpenter Road through the trees.

A quarter mile away, glittering surface of Round Pond which was too large to be called a pond yet not large enough to be called a lake.

Stare and stare from an upstairs window and forget how awful humanity is. (Aunt Traci said.)

Eventually the property would be hers but in the meantime the will had stalled in probate court, which was understaffed in Shaheen County and poorly administered.

She was little Miriam's aunt after all. Older sister of the (irresponsible) father.

Damned good thing Lew hadn't had other kids. (That anyone knew about.) Just not reliable.

Miriam was eight years old. They called her Meer-me.

She would remember that her birthday had been just a few days before this. Her aunt had made her an angel food cake covered in that stiff white sugary frosting she loved.

The kind of sugar rush, your mouth hurts. Tears flood your eyes.

Eight little pink candles on the cake. Eight little flames to be blown out. (Meer-me did not blow out all the candles with a single breath.) But there was no one else to eat the cake—just Aunt Traci and Meer-me.

Her third birthday since she'd come to live with her aunt.

Once, she'd overheard Aunt Traci on the phone late at night. Laughing, complaining. She'd had to break into the house, Traci was telling a woman friend. Nobody would give her the goddamned key.

Lowering her voice to say that Meer-me was doing okay . . . considering.

Meer-me was her name within the family. But Miriam Frances was her name at school.

Aunt Traci was telling her friend that she had all she could do to keep herself alive now that she had her brother and sister-in-law's daughter to take care of, could you believe it? Cleaning up after Lew's messes. Practically had to beg, borrow, steal money for groceries.

No idea where they are. I doubt they are together. Nicola is hiding from him, maybe.

You bet I am! Keeping a record of every penny spent on that child. The damned parents owe me.

Meer-me is stunned, hearing such words. Harsh, jeering. How is this possible—her aunt Traci, who is so nice to her, who cries over her, speaking of her in such a way?

Her heart is broken. She is running away from Aunt Traci. Never, ever coming back to Aunt Traci.

Following the path at the edge of the pasture. Along the shallow creek.

Running in high grasses, stinging thistles. Seeing with angry satisfaction blood oozing from thin cuts on her arms and legs.

She will hide in the pinewoods. She will hide amid the big sun-bleached boulders in the creek bed, smelly and discolored from bird droppings. Flocks of yellow finches in the creek bed that rise into the air when she approaches.

Elsewhere, crows, blackbirds. Brown-winged hawks, turkey vultures.

She knows what a turkey vulture is. She has been told, if you are alive, a vulture will not harm you.

A smell of something mineral, and a stronger smell of rot. Dying and dead things in the creek bed—small fish, crabs. If you dug through the pebbles, mucky soil. The stillness in the air like a sharply indrawn breath as she approached the creek.

Because she'd said *yes.* Which was a lie, and she knew what a lie was, but she uttered the lie that could never be retracted. And so there came from that lie—the lie of a frightened five-year-old who'd wanted to please Daddy—what she would see in the tall grasses in the country-side north of Shaheen when she was eight years old.

She would not forgive Mommy, for Mommy had seemed to love her best. She would forgive Daddy, for Daddy could not help himself, he'd been *driven away from his home.*

And where had they gone? No one knew.

She knew. Bones scattered in the tall grasses. The Daddy-skull, the Mommy-skull.

Her eyes see. *She* does not see, her eyes see.

Her mouth begins screaming. Not Meer-me screaming, but her mouth.

Saw but didn't see. She'd learn to unsee.
Bones in the grass. Just—scattered.
Looking like animal bones. At first.

But no. A shape to it: (human) skeleton.

No. Two (human) skeletons.

Rotted clothing, a single rotted shoe looking like it is mid-kick.

Too soon in her life. She is only a child of eight.

Too young to know the word *skeleton.*

Her face smarts from sunburn. Her eyes are fiery in their sockets, and she will never, ever be able to close her eyes again . . .

The bones are everywhere in the tall grasses. Her eyes are frantic not to see, but she sees.

Bones have been carried downstream in the creek. Caught amid rocks, boulders. Sun-bleached and as bright as shouts.

Terrified of stepping on the bones. No!

It is very bad to step on the bones, for the bones are helpless in the tall grass where they have fallen or been dragged. Though she is only eight years old, she knows this.

As she recognizes the Daddy-skull, which is peering up at her.

You! What'd I tell you, Princess.

Did you think I'd forget you?

And here is the Mommy-skull, pleading.

Oh honey—I didn't leave you. I never left you . . .

In horror she sees: finger bones, mixed together.

She sees: something gleaming in the grass. Is it a ring?—a small ring, a badly tarnished silver ring with a pale, cracked stone.

And now she sees: the ugly, rusted things for

which she has not (yet) a name, too young to know the name, which will come to her years later while watching a crime program on TV in her aunt Traci's house in Chautauqua Falls.

Handcuffs.

Testimony

What am I seeing? My father?—I think that man is my father . . .

It is true as people say, my father is very handsome. And his smile—you want to see that smile.

You do not want to see a man frown. Any man, but especially a tall handsome father.

His name is Llewyn Hayman, but I didn't know this at the time. I knew him as Daddy.

I can see Daddy, but he can't see me—why is that?

"Love Love Love
My Little Meer-Me Like Crazy"

It must be a very special occasion. Daddy returns home unexpected and tells the babysitter that her services are no longer needed, he'll be home the rest of the day, what's he owe her?—and the girl stammers, saying Nicola will pay her, and Daddy says, "No. I guess you didn't hear me. I said— *I'm* paying you."

When the child and Daddy are alone together, Daddy lowers himself from his high height like a man climbing down a ladder. Grunting, laughing in that way that signals there's nothing funny, yes, but Daddy is going to laugh because Daddy is a good sport, squatting, lowering himself to the four-year-old's height. Christ!—his knees are aching, shrapnel fragments deep embedded in the flesh of the right thigh, slow working their way to the surface of the rough, ribbed skin. But Daddy is smiling, smiling hard, smiling happy, gazing into the child's eyes exactly at eye level.

The child is shy of her Daddy, who is new in her life. Hardly a year in her life. (Though the child is too young to calculate units of time beyond today, tomorrow, next week.) She'd been born (Mommy explained to her) while Daddy was away in the army, fighting to protect her and all other children from harm, and when Daddy returned to live with her and Mommy, she did not know him for a while and was afraid of him for a while, but not now, for she knows him now, he is her Daddy who loves her very much.

Though it is strange that Daddy has returned home so early from work. While Mommy is still at work.

Saying, in the kind-Daddy voice, "Does Mommy have a friend who visits her when Daddy is away?"

The child sucks at her fingers, not knowing what to say, because Mommy has more than one friend. To say that Mommy has one friend is not right.

The child sucks at her fingers, not knowing what to say, because Mommy's friends are (mostly) women who come often to the house, but Daddy knows these women, so it is confusing what Daddy is asking her, if Daddy already knows the answer.

The child is further confused because Daddy's breath smells like sweet rotted peaches. It is a Daddy-smell she has come to recognize, and it is not always a good smell.

"Sweetie, just tell Daddy: Does Mommy have *a special friend* who visits her when Daddy is away?"

Not sure what Daddy wants her to say. His fingers gripping her shoulders, not (yet) shaking her, but she has learned to steel herself for the sudden shake, not (always) an angry shake, could be just impatience, exasperation. Annoying to an adult when a child who is getting too old for such behavior sucks at her fingers. In fact Daddy slaps her fingers from her mouth, not a hard slap, not a slap to hurt, just a chiding Daddy-slap of the kind Mommy makes too sometimes, a *love slap.*

"A *special friend*—male. Does she?"

Male. The child isn't sure what this means, exactly.

Before Daddy's smile fades entirely, the child murmurs "Uh-huh." Shakes her head *yes.*

"Right! Exactly what I thought."

Daddy laughs, rocking back on his heels. Daddy makes a whistling sound.

"*Fucking* exactly what I thought."

The child is released by Daddy's fingers. The child is eager to know whether Daddy is happy with her now.

But with an aggrieved grunt—(his knees! legs! back!—Christ!)—Daddy climbs back up to his high height.

The child is left behind, staring after Daddy as he stomps to the rear of the house. Laughing, cursing—"Let's do a little forensic investigating, let's see what we've got here"—tearing open the bed (which Mommy made that morning with the child's help), examining the sheets, pillowcases, switching on a bedside lamp so he can see better, crouched over the bedclothes, sniffing, checking for stains, stray hairs, suspicious hairs, and in the bathroom stooping to examine the shower drain where incriminating evidence may have gathered. Laughing as if, finally, he is very happy, as Daddy is not always so happy, but (the child understands) he *wants very badly to be happy, happiness is Daddy's truest self.*

The child has trailed after Daddy, uncertain. The child registers that he has (more or less) forgotten her. But she cannot gauge if she should remind him that she is still there, or if she should not interfere with Daddy, whose face is flushed and excited, whose eyes are alert and awake, as if there are loud noises close about his head, distracting him.

In the bedroom Daddy yanks open bureau drawers, lets them fall to the floor. Mommy's underwear, nightgowns. Yanks open the closet door, runs his hand roughly through clothes on hangers, knocking some to the floor. Kicking at shoes.

The child tries not to be frightened. The child is shy in Daddy's presence. Yet she wants Daddy's eyes to move onto her. *She hopes to be pretty enough.*

On his way out of the house, Daddy catches sight of the child, abashed and uncertain in a corner of the kitchen.

"Hey there, kid—Meer-me."

Meer-me is a baby-name. The child knows that

her name is Miriam—*M'riam*. Adults call her either name, depending on their mood.

Daddy stoops over her, clumsily. His face is beaded with sweat, like oily raindrops. Daddy is breathing harshly, as if he has just climbed a flight of stairs. Doesn't take time to squat on his heels again, but stoops over her, the rotted-peach smell strong in her nostrils, and hastily bestows hot, wet, rough Daddy-kisses on her face, telling her that Daddy *loves loves loves his little Meer-me like crazy.*

Daddy disappears out the door, and the door slams behind him. His sweat-smell lingers.

Then he reappears at the door. Jubilantly calling to the child where she stands dazed in a corner of the kitchen, "Tell Mommy—Daddy was here, and Daddy left. Tell Mommy—*Daddy knows.*"

Testimony

And so I know—it was my fault.

What happened to my mother, my fault.

But no one ever blamed me. Mommy never blamed me.

Mommy never knew.

Reconnoiter

Where is she?—it's 7:13 p.m. Waiting for the (estranged) wife for forty-five minutes at least.

In the Ford Warrior, tinted glass on all windows and sides, dull-gleaming pewter like a tank.

And headlights cut. Of course.

Parked near the corner. Three houses up from her/their house at 388 Grant. Easy to turn the ignition, escape if he's sighted.

Flashlight. Binoculars in his lap. Dark jacket, dark visor cap pulled low over his forehead. Hiking boots.

No weapon, but in his pocket, in pink tissue paper, a little present for his daughter. Since he'd missed her—is it fifth?—birthday.

Six-pack of beer on the passenger's seat beside him. Cracking open the third, or maybe the fourth. Lukewarm, not great tasting. But might as well finish the pack.

The (estranged) wife has never seen this vehicle. It's new, rented.

Advantage of rental cars, SUVs, pickups—he never has the same vehicle for more than a few days. No one gets habituated to the sight of it. If the (estranged) wife happens to notice a vehicle on Grant Street, or slow-passing her on the highway, or turning into the mall parking lot just behind her, or idling at the edge of the parking lot behind her office building at the community college, she won't see it a second time.

A way of *keeping in motion* even when (like now) he is patiently sitting/waiting.

Also, the (estranged) wife may have reason to believe that he is (still) out of town.

Possibly hospitalized. (*She'd* like that!)

Since she expelled him from the house. From his life.

The house, the wife, the child—these are his life.

In the army, in combat, in the military hospital, telling himself that if he returned home, if God spared him and he returned home to this house on Grant Street, Chautauqua Falls, to the wife, the daughter, *his* wife and *his* daughter, he would be the best goddamned husband and dad there is. Never drink again, or anyway not to excess. Never get high again, because to get high is to damage your chances for living, enduring, in the shithole world without being high. *That* is the great challenge.

He has been parked here at the corner of Grant and Pearce since 6:30 p.m. Made the decision last night, unable to sleep. Stinging red ants in the bed, felt like. Could not get comfortable. Could not stop itching. No refill from the VA to assure that he'd sleep (maybe) three hours. Lower body, buttocks throbbing with pain. Guts seething. She'd threatened *injunction.* She'd threatened accusing him of *molesting our daughter.*

If he follows her. Tries to see her (again). Tries to speak with his daughter on a (week) day not an official custody day (weekend).

Or just calling her. Calling and leaving messages. That's against the law? In a free country? Calling an (estranged, not divorced) wife? Leaving messages? *Hello, Nicola? Please don't hang up. I only want to talk, and I won't talk long. I promise . . .*

Unfair and unjust. *Injunction!* Could not believe she would go to a judge, charging such lies. After all they'd meant to each other. After the daughter they both cherished.

Still stunning to him, too much to absorb: she'd actually threatened him, if he didn't *back off,* to charge him with "improperly" touching their daughter.

When he caught her cheating. Total shock, surprise to him.

She is the adulterer, not him. *She* is the one having an affair. So tell the big lie. That's what women do. Hire a lawyer.

(Ever notice, he'd asked the asshole, how close *lawyer* is to *liar?*)

Worst thing you can accuse a father of. *Sex molestation, rape.*

Of his own little daughter!

So what if it isn't true. Her word against his. Meer-me is an impressionable little girl. If Nicola insists that Daddy touched her where he wasn't supposed to touch her, giving her a bath (for instance), dressing her, hugging her, eventually Nicola will triumph, since Nicola has custody of Meer-me five days out of seven.

A mother is always believed. They will believe me. Meer-me will believe me. If you don't back off, you will regret it.

Even if you never go to jail you will be so shamed in this town, you will have to leave. I am warning you!

And so he'd backed off. If a shotgun is aimed at his face, for sure a man is going to back off.

Licking his wounds, considering. He'd been putting pressure on her to grant him more custody time with the daughter, and this is her revenge. Unless he can prove that Nicola is lying, threatening him . . . He'd have to record her gloating over the phone, needling him, but how can he do that?—she refuses to speak with him.

Unless he can convince the daughter to defend him. Accuse Mommy of lying. Of coaxing Meer-me to say *Daddy touched me here. And here . . .*

But five is too young. Scared and skittish, not trusting either her Daddy or (he guesses) her Mommy, a child so young could not begin to discern truth from lies. The most recent parent who'd spoken to her would be the parent she believed, and the most recent would be Nicola.

(Maybe gather proof of Nicola's promiscuous

behavior to present to a family court judge? Record conversations with his iPhone with mutual friends, acquaintances, coworkers of Nicola's at the college? If she has been misusing drugs, and what kind of drugs. If she has been observed drunk. Especially if she has been observed driving with their daughter while impaired . . . The risk would be if it got back to Nicola, as possibly it would, providing her with more evidence to use against *him*.)

(Anonymously, he might alert local police; supply them with his wife's name, license plate number, year and make of her car, street address—*A child's life may be endangered. Suspected negligent/abusive mother.*)

(But this is risky, too. Might backfire if police found out who he was.)

The wisest new strategy is, give Nicola more money each month than the family court judge has mandated.

This will placate her. Not immediately, but in time. Seeing that the (estranged) husband is deferential to her, not threatening.

Seeing that he (still) loves her.

Ashamed to confess, no he is *not ashamed* to confess—still loves the woman who has betrayed him.

He'd served his country. Their families had been proud of him. She'd been proud of him then. Crazy for him in his dress uniform. Everybody admires you in your dress uniform. Military posture like there's a rod up your back keeping you from caving in.

And now he's been abandoned by his country. Sucker!

Sympathy for the dead who never came back, so nobody has to give a damn about them, but what about *him?* His mistake is, he'd come back.

Because he wasn't so damaged as some others. His skull, his hair, you could see tracks in his scalp through his hair, but his face is (mostly) untouched, just a few scars on his cheeks (women love to touch with their fingertips, tongues). Hadn't lost a tooth like a friend, missing his lower jaw after a roadside bomb.

Well, he'd had two (rotten) teeth removed by an army dentist before he was even shipped out. (Still waiting for the implants he'd been promised.) But hadn't lost a tooth in combat.

Maybe if he'd lost an eye? A leg? Spine twisted, he's in a wheelchair? Would the (estranged) wife have remained faithful to him?

Doubt it. Deceitful.

Probably, though he can't prove it, she'd started screwing other guys while he'd been away in fucking Iraq. Questions he'd asked of their friends, they'd sounded guarded answering.

Left his weapon at home. Purposely.

Even the hunting knife. (But there is always

a knife on the premises, and wherever you find yourself, there are premises.)

Fact is, Nicola has always been weak. Leaning on him, as a weak person does, when she'd needed him, casting him off when he'd needed her.

Breaks your heart, your own wife won't drive you to the VA hospital.

Needing mainly a refill for his meds. Checking the shrapnel fragments in his thigh. Checking (possible) pinched nerve in his back. Headaches. (Blood clots?) Previous time he'd (also) had to drive alone, they hadn't even been separated yet, but Nicola claimed she was too busy, nor was there anyone in his family—pretending to be sympathetic with him, but when it comes to helping him out—fuck *them*. Waited four hours, but at least a doctor saw him, or someone saw him, could've been an intern, gave him the refill, which was all he really wanted.

Not sure the guy was a doctor. Staring into a computer most of the time, scarcely glanced at *Lew Hayman*. That expression in the (Asian) face of something like contempt. Bastard would've shuddered if the patient had reached out to touch *him*.

Hey! Look at me. Here's me.

I am the patient here. Me!

Not that he wants more tests. He *does not* want more tests.

Halfway into the fMRI, fucking thing broke

down. That's what they told him. Reschedule, except they never did.

Could have a brain tumor. Fuck they care.

This time, seven fucking hours. Waiting room full. He'd walked out, finally. Told the assholes what he thought on the way out, and by the time he got to the front entrance sliding door, there's two fat-assed security guards waiting to escort him the rest of the way.

Picked up a six-pack to drink on the long drive back.

Meds don't seriously help, only just muffle. Had enough of fucking *muffle*.

That was Buffalo, two-hour drive north on the Thruway if you maintain a speed of seventy.

Faster than that, too risky. Llewyn Hayman's driver's license is suspended and any excuse he'd give the trooper, such as *My wife can't take time out to drive me,* would get a laugh in the face.

Most of what happened to him in the military he has forgotten. Shock and awe they'd called it. Whose shock and whose awe? But keeping an exit clear for your escape, the way he has now, parked near the intersection with Pearce, that he remembers.

Matter of life or death. How you position yourself. See the enemy before they see you. No second chances.

Grant is a narrow, potholed street at the eastern

edge of Chautauqua Falls. Brick rowhouses along one side of the street, small bungalows on the other. *His* house is one of the bungalows.

Bungalow!—goddamned condescending word.

He'd wanted to make a down payment on a small but stylish-looking ranch house in a newer part of town, a little more than they could afford. Nicola could borrow money from her family, except Nicola hadn't wanted to borrow money from her family, preferred the clapboard *bungalow* because it was more within their price range and their daughter could walk to an elementary school nearby, eventually.

He'd gotten to like it okay. Tidy little house they'd fixed up inside. Painting walls together, putting down linoleum tile. Baby's crib. Silver stars across the ceiling. Jesus, he'd been happy there! Until.

No baby now. Not-so-little girl. It's weird how fast they grow.

(Yes, he'd checked her out. Her tiny hairless vagina. No harm in it. Bathing her. Nicola said not to bother, Meer-me could go without a bath, even two baths, maybe don't take the trouble. Nicola was sounding weird about this, he should have realized. Thinking the absolute worst about a man, a father. Even when they'd still been okay together, making love together, at least some-times. Even then.)

Time: 7:31 p.m.

By now Meer-me would've had supper. He misses meals with her even if, when he tries to recall them, he can't.

Tonight Nicola must be having dinner with—who?

He'd cruised by the community college before coming here, through the parking lot. Her car hadn't been there.

Lights in the house. Blinds pulled down to the windowsills. As if the occupants are fearful that someone might peer into their windows.

As if Lew Hayman would creep up to his own house to peer into his own windows like a Peeping Tom! LIke a pervert! One more insult he's had to endure since she asked him to move out, no explanation.

But why? Tell me why.

You know why.

Not meeting his eye. Ashamed to admit she'd been screwing this other guy, who knows how long.

Ashamed to acknowledge that without him, her lawful husband, there'd be no *bungalow* at 388 Grant Street for her to live in. Without him, Jesus, there'd be no Meer-me.

Not much traffic on Grant. Which is good.

Kids in the neighborhood for Meer-me to play with. Nicola thought that was important since Meer-me is an only child.

Only child. One of a kind.

Except kids today don't play outside as they'd once done. As *he'd* done.

Grew up on the old farm in Shaheen. As a kid he'd hated the countryside, hated the (deadly, boring, failing) farm, but it was a time in his life when he could wander without adult supervision. Tramping for miles in the woods along the shallow rocky creek, through the churchyard, into the marshy fields. Hitchhiking on country roads, getting rides into town.

He'd tried to get Nicola to camp out with him in the woods at Round Pond. Deciduous trees. Soft, grassy earth. In school he'd liked to boast to classmates that he went hunting with his (male) relatives, shot his first deer at eleven, though that hadn't happened, exactly.

Not so great with guns. In training, Lew Hayman never scored as high as he'd wanted.

Maybe he'd shot (some of) the (Iraqi) enemy. So much confusion, he never knew. Fired his weapon, who knows where the bullets went. More than once it was kids they were shooting at, no more than thirteen years old. Moving targets. Just followed orders like everybody else, but even then sometimes he didn't—not much.

Not proud of himself. Best to forget. The other vets in Chautauqua Falls were not so friendly, or they were weirdos you wouldn't want to befriend. Like guys at the VA, waiting like him. He'd start to nod off, confused. Maybe he was back

106

in the blazing-sand hell? In a hospital there?

Asshole, d'you think just 'cause you're dead, we're finished with you?

Headlights approaching. But not hers.

Still, he's reacting. Stimulus-response. Dry-mouthed, heart-kick, rush of adrenaline.

In group therapy they were instructed to tell themselves calmly at such times *You are not in a combat zone. You are no longer a soldier. You are a civilian, you are at peace. No one is trying to kill you. You are not trying to kill anyone. You are not in uniform. You are back home.*

Tell yourself *One breath at a time. One breath at a time.*

And breathe deeply, slowly. Let the adrenaline rush fade. Observe the rapid heartbeat, how it becomes calm, tame. Under your control.

Sometimes, this works. Not always.

That adrenaline rush!—like coming, except it's the heart.

Maybe it was a mistake, leaving his weapon back at his place. Debated over bringing it, but— *No. You are a civilian now.*

He does have a permit for a concealed handgun. Honorable discharge from the U.S. Armed Forces and background check okay.

But the knife. Eight-inch stainless steel. Had since he was a kid out in Shaheen, might've slipped it into the glove compartment of the Ford Warrior just in case.

But, well—he'd debated. Decided *no.*

Is Nicola late? He has the idea, not sure why, fixed in his head like shrapnel fragments that can't be picked out, that she was supposed to be back home by seven p.m.—which makes her almost an hour late.

That job of hers! Pretending to give a shit about teaching remedial English to foreigners. Pretending to consider it a *career.*

Leaving his little girl with the Haitian woman. Six-foot-tall black female cutting those shiny cobra eyes at him—*voodoo.*

Christ, he's afraid of that one. What's the name—Dominique.

They see through you. Eviscerate you. Voodoo blade at the scrotum, slicing a man wide open so his guts spill out. And the white bitch laughing— *You go, girl!*

The wife's claim will be the job (again). After she has promised to be a better mother.

Meaning, *more loving to our (neglected) daughter.*

Meaning, *home at least half the time.*

Meaning, *not fucking her boss.*

Meaning, *not fucking whoever she picks up at the Pit Stop, Stroth's, Marriott, Mediterra, etc.*

Meaning, *having the courtesy and fundamental decency to provide the (estranged) husband a lie plausible enough for him to believe without surrendering the last bit of his self-respect even as she is (certainly) fucking her boss and whoever else.*

Blood is accelerating through the sinewy tunnels of his body. Thawing out the numbness he's been enduring for too long. Feels good!

His minister friend Ned Clark has told him, forgiving your wife for having betrayed you is the beginning of wisdom. You may not think so now, but looking back at this time, you will. And more important, she will.

And the child, Miriam. *She* will recall her daddy kindly.

Met Ned Clark at Small World Coffee. First glance, you'd take Ned for some kind of hippie, long hair, wispy beard, loose-fitting clothes, benevolent smile, turns out he's assistant chaplain at the university. Has a degree from Union Theological Seminary plus a master's in psychology.

Yes. I will forgive you, Nicola.

For the sake of the child but also—for the sake of our love.

That's the shameful part. He still loves her. Despite.

One thing, they'd grown up together. Had the kid together.

Before the birth, they'd shared some experiences not everyone knows about in their families. *He* will never tell.

Though he did confide in Ned Clark. Saw the look in Ned's face of surprise, dismay. But being the guy he is, an actual Christian, said he wasn't one to judge, had no comment on what Lew was telling him other than to wish he hadn't heard it, for (as Ned made clear) he had no way of corroborating it, and he'd learned as a counselor never to hear just one side of a story.

Fair enough, the (estranged) husband concurs. Though it isn't likely the (estranged) wife would admit to having done such a thing, is it?

You could say.

Known the woman eleven years, more or less. Been with her for at least eight of those years. Mistake was to get married. (She'd said.) So it has seemed.

He's a romantic, sentimentalist. He's the one who'd wanted to be married.

Wanted kids. Three, four kids.

Settled for one, who'd barely made it.

Hoping to hell, he'd told Ned Clark, that their beautiful little daughter will never know how Daddy had to plead with her mother not to have an abortion instead of carrying the pregnancy to term. How many nights sitting up with Nicola, trying to reason with her. Going through a six-pack like it was nothing. Helping the woman through her fear of pregnancy, fear of her (sexual) body being deformed, fear of the agony of childbirth.

Frankly, he'd thought it was ninety-nine percent female vanity. A sexually attractive female is appalled at the prospect of losing her sex appeal to men.

The swell of the (female) belly. Can hardly walk, waddle. Nicola confessed how, as a girl, she'd looked quickly away from the sight of a pregnant woman, couldn't bear to see. And her own mother pregnant at age forty, swollen ankles, varicose veins, sweaty and panting.

No, no!—she just didn't want to endure it, not yet.

One thing is clear, the pregnancy was an accident. Which is to say, a miracle.

Impulsively he'd said he wished *he* could have the baby instead of her but that turned out to be not a great thing to say, for Nicola recoiled, laughing, cursing like a madwoman, trying to hit him, claw his face. Until he had no choice but to grab her wrists, try to hold her still.

Hard to blame her, he'd supposed. The female body is so *physical.* Like a snake, sinuous and supple, smooth-skinned, insatiable at times, frenzied with desire. A man is not like that. In the male, desire is not ignoble. There is not such raw need. The male is the warrior of desire, the female the (passive) object.

The one fills the other with his seed. The female is the vessel.

Sex-desire like a luminous flame playing over

her body. Her eyes rolled back in their sockets, she cried, wept, had no idea what words she uttered, that sometimes astounding him, but provoking him as well, so that in making love to the woman he might find himself making love to many women, and all of them strangers to him.

But after becoming pregnant she'd begun to push him from her. *No, no! Haven't you done enough. I hate you!*

Of course she didn't mean it. Later apologizing. Not knowing what she said. Like speaking in tongues.

It was *alien life* inside her, she said. Could feel it thinking, plotting. *Alien life* sucking at her own.

For days, nights, weeks they'd discussed abortion. To her it was *the abortion,* to him it was *an abortion.*

He'd said, we will do what you want to do, Nicola. Your body is yours, no one should tell you what to do.

Fuck you, she'd said. That is exactly what you are doing—telling me what to do.

No. No. No it is not. He'd pleaded for understanding. We will do what you choose. I promise.

And that was so, except: he could not stop thinking about the baby, their baby, not an idea or a theory, but an actual being, an embryo, already in existence.

His baby. (Why not admit it? *His* DNA. Not just *hers*.)

Those early weeks of the pregnancy, his wife had been so emotional, so moody, frequently threatening to kill herself. He'd had a fantasy of acquiring a pair of handcuffs to cuff their wrists together so he'd know exactly where she was at any given time.

Not very practical, however. Since he had to work.

Not sure he'd ever really talked her out of an abortion. Or even suicide, which would have been, for the pregnant woman, a sort of suicide-homicide combination. (Had that poet woman committed suicide-homicide? The one Nicola was always quoting?) But in time, Nicola forgot. Became more involved in the pregnancy, got to know other expectant mothers, planned for the baby's birth, making lists of names.

Miriam Frances. A (deceased) grandmother of Nicola's he'd never met. Not his favorite name for a little girl—Miriam! But they could call her Meer-me.

Checks his watch: 7:43 p.m. Still not home!

Must be with a man. The boss, the supervisor—possibly. But there have been others, he knows.

Ned Clark advises: Don't accuse her. Don't drag up the past. Nothing is gained by recrimination.

He has told Ned Clark about the (estranged) wife's infidelities. But he has not told Ned Clark about the (estranged) wife blackmailing him with the threat of an accusation that he'd "improperly" touched his own daughter.

The most powerful weapon wielded by a wife, a mother. Making war upon the (estranged) husband. Just the hint of sex molestation, rape, incest—Lew Hayman would be destroyed.

He understands, Nicola can't help herself. She has been trying to break a habit of drinking too much, taking more medication than she is pre-scribed, losing her temper with Meer-me.

Bipolar disorder in her family. From what he'd heard, at least two relatives of hers, on her mother's side, have committed suicide.

Though he is the *wounded vet,* he will not play that card. For he is healthier than Nicola, essentially.

Mentally, physically. Spiritually.

Meer-me is happiest with Daddy, that has been obvious to both father and mother. The mother's revenge, to accuse an affectionate father of some-thing terrible.

He has always been the magnanimous one; he can forgive.

Back in high school, with his friends, he'd been the one to take charge. In the early years of the marriage he'd naturally been the more confident, stronger. He is not emotional, though he is *feeling.* He is capable of envisioning the future in a way an emotionally blinded individual cannot. Finishes the last of the lukewarm beer. Sour, belching taste in his mouth.

He will speak with the (estranged) wife calmly. Not in the presence of glaring Dominique. Not in the presence of Meer-me. Preferably in private.

In the bedroom that was theirs, he'd painted the walls and ceiling robin's egg blue, which dried darker than they'd expected. Not realizing that you don't paint a ceiling.

That is, a ceiling should be painted white. Who knew?

Well, they'd had a discussion about it. Nicola had thought no, a ceiling is usually white; Lew had insisted, a ceiling may be "usually" white but is not inevitably white.

But robin's egg blue walls and ceiling were too much. The ceiling, oppressive.

He'd known, but had put off repainting. What difference did it make (he'd reasoned), most of their time in bed was at night; it did not greatly matter if the ceiling was white or blue. But Nicola insisted, the ceiling would have to be repainted.

Finally he'd returned home one night, and the bedroom ceiling had been painted creamy white. Nicola was proud of herself. She'd painted the ceiling with a roller, a bandana covering her hair.

Isn't it much improved? Before, it was like one of those prisoner-of-war cages with a low ceiling.

They'd laughed together. In those days.

If he could get her into that room, just once. Both of them calm, soft-speaking.

Steadying her hands. If she doesn't flinch away—kissing her hands.

As once, not long ago, the husband kissed the wife all over her hot, pulsing skin. And she'd loved it.

Now it's 7:55 p.m. Too excited, too restless to remain in the vehicle. Decides to get out, stretch his legs.

Flashlight in one pocket, binoculars in the other. With his dark clothing he is a walking/gliding shadow.

No one on the street. No one watching at any window visible to him.

Makes his way casually along the sidewalk. At the driveway beside the bungalow, turns in. His heart has begun to accelerate, it's a sweet sensation.

A man turning into the driveway of his house. *His.*

Along the side of the house, overgrown bushes. Some kind of sweet white blossoms in the spring that Nicola had liked. Wedding wreath? *Bridal* wreath?

The injustice of it—his predicament, his life—sweeps over him like a torrent of scalding steam. That he has been banned from his own house under the terms of a "separation" to which he'd agreed only reluctantly, under duress—that his only, beloved child is a few yards away from him inside the house, in the care of a hostile stranger.

Decides not to knock at the door. Not yet just. Better strategy is to reconnoiter.

Circles the house. He knows the terrain. Stealthily makes his way. The disadvantage of drawn blinds is, the occupants of the house can't see outside.

As he recalls, close beside the house, inside the canopy of bushes, there is grassless earth, soft from recent rain. He must walk deliberately, his boots sink into the soil.

If he wanted, he could force open a cellar window. If he was (ever) that desperate.

Force the window when no one is home. Return later, in the night, make his way to the child's room, gently wake her, press his finger over her lips to quiet her, wrap her in a blanket, in his arms, carry her out of the house and into his life. By the time the (estranged) wife woke in the morning, Daddy and Meer-me are *in the wind.*

Or, make his way in the night to the (estranged) wife's bedroom, formerly *his* bedroom . . .

In the compartments of his brain, like a honeycomb, he relocates these possibilities. He will revisit them later, in a quieter time.

Presses his ear against one of the windows. A voice inside? Voices?

Actual voices, or TV?—hard to judge.

Tries to peer through a crack in the interior blind, but can't make anything out.

Still, he knows that Meer-me is inside. He is eager to see her. He'd missed their last weekend, unavoidably. Late in calling to cancel, the little girl had been waiting for Daddy for an hour, maybe more, Nicola was furious with him on the phone. *How can you do this to her! It's pathetic enough how she stands by the window.*

Pisses him off, how Nicola thinks she can scream at him. How, sensing a weakness, a female will pounce.

Should Daddy tap on the window?—Meer-me will know who it is.

All Daddy wants is a hug, a fleeting kiss. All Daddy wants is to know he is *loved*.

Daddy has a present for little Miriam, a mother-of-pearl barrette wrapped in pink tissue paper. Since Daddy missed her birthday and Mommy was so fierce to him, he didn't feel welcome to bring it over at the time.

But the nanny would interfere. Tall, ferocious Haitian female.

It's her voice he hears. (He thinks.) Mildly chiding, scolding.

He feels a sensation of pure rage for the woman. Recalling her arrogance toward him in the past.

First met Dominique when Nicola hired her unilaterally, without consulting him, to babysit Meer-me five days a week after she'd returned to work. The way the woman stared at him for a beat or two before smiling.

That look of assessing, judging.

Lew Hayman is a good-looking (white) man, used to seeing females expressing interest in him, smiling at him, but this (black) female is letting him know she doesn't think much of him.

He isn't a racist. Certainly, he is not. Hung out with black guys in the army. Got along just fine. And Hispanics. (Asians, not so much. Doesn't trust Asians, they're too smart.)

Actually, he feels magnanimity, generosity. For all the races.

Though repelled by fat women, any race. Mannish women. Any color skin. Big, floppy breasts, belly and hips—repulsive. The slovenliness of it. He's not the kind of guy turned on by female flesh in itself, without an attractive face, personality.

Dominique calmly assessing him, six feet tall female with biceps, muscled legs, crew-cut hair.

Think I give a shit what you feel about me? Stick your white dick somewhere else.

(Or maybe he has imagined this. Hostility in black faces, eyes!)

(As if they are peering into the (white) man's soul.)

Makes his way to the rear of the house. Backyard dissolves into shadows. There's a swing set that came with the house, he'd painted.

Strange, Daddy is exiled out here. Not right.

As usual, the garage door isn't shut. Serves Nicola right—a visitor to the premises can step inside.

Here, Lew uses the flashlight sparingly. In case someone happens to be watching or Nicola suddenly turns into the driveway.

What's he looking for? Nothing seems much changed. Last time he'd been in the garage, a few months ago. Cardboard boxes in stacks. Trash cans. Not looking for a hammer, though (he recalls) there are at least two hammers in the toolbox.

Crowbar.

Finds it where he'd last seen it, propped against a wall. Picks it up, weighs it in his hand. Just in case.

Self-defense. Never know when you will need to defend yourself.

He'd killed men in Iraq, he thinks. Possibly women, children. Couldn't be sure. But no one up close, whose face he'd actually seen.

Some guys, the way they'd boasted. Laughing like loons. But not him.

Nicola had tried to get him to talk to her when he first came home. But he'd had medical problems, distractions. Buzz in his ears. Headaches.

Self-medicating it's called. No one to blame.

Somehow, since the army, even before he'd been sent to the war, he'd lost his ability to "talk" as people do. As he recalls having done when he was younger.

It's something you take for granted—talking. Like falling asleep when you're tired.

But you can lose that ability. Talk—sleep. Just forget how.

Still, Nicola persisted. As if she knew him better than he knew himself, as if there were some magic word or phrase or kiss or caress that would transform him to what he'd been before. But no.

Lew, what has happened to you? I know it's hard—but—you can tell me. Please.

It was a natural question, he supposed. From a woman, a wife. He understood that. But frankly, it was none of anybody's business, and especially not hers.

At a little distance from himself, that sensation of being an apparatus, like a TV set, not a new-model TV, but an older, foursquare and heavy floor model. And the screen grainy, fuzzy. *His* brain, inside his (broken, tired) body.

You could turn the TV on or off. Or someone could. Voices chattering out of the box. You could mute the voices. Someone could.

Seeing himself and the woman in bed together from across the room. Weird! Wild. How people make themselves vulnerable to attack by removing their clothes, lying down horizontally.

He's been standing in a trance, thinking. But—about what?

Can't recall. Rouses himself: crowbar in his hand.

His strategy will be to knock at the front door. Speak politely to the woman. See how it goes.

The crowbar—he hides it in the bushes beside the door. Just in case.

Brushes back his hair from his forehead, replaces the dark visor cap. Draws his hands across his jaws, feels stubble. Christ!

Not sure what he looks like. Last few days. Totally forgot to shave, shower. Change his socks. He's been sleeping in his clothes. But he isn't drunk, and he isn't high. Can't be faulted on those counts.

Knocks on the front door, louder and more aggressive than he'd expected.

No answer. Sudden silence inside.

Knocks a second time, less loudly. Politely.

Hesitantly the door is opened. Not quite far enough for the man who happens to be the co-owner of the house to step inside.

He is pleasant, affable. Ignoring the startled, hostile stare of the black woman.

"H'lo? Is it—Dominique? We've met, I'm Miriam's dad. May I—"

He moves to step inside, but Dominique deftly blocks him.

"Mr. Hayman—"

"We've met: I'm Lew."

"—Nicola told me, if you showed up—no."

Sees that Dominique is wary of him. Dominique has been prepared.

"What do you mean—showed up? What the fuck does that mean? This is my house, I live here . . ."

"I am sorry, mister. I have to close the door now."

The woman speaks boldly, bravely, but he sees that indeed she is afraid of him. Goddamn she's tall—his height, or nearly. Him in his hiking boots, her in sneakers.

Still pleasant, still smiling, he insists he has a right to come inside the house, for the house is his, as she well knows. And little Miriam is his. And the black woman says in a quavering voice that he does not have the right, that there has been a separation agreement, Nicola has explained. Another time she declares she is going to shut the door, and another time he tries to prevent her, booted foot in the door. Still, he is smiling. This black bitch better be grateful. If Hayman stops smiling, she is going to be in a world of hurt, and fast.

"I was just bringing Meer-me a little present, a birthday present. I had to miss her birthday last week . . . Meer-me? Sweetie? Where is she?"

Dominique hesitates. White-rimmed eyes the size of a horse's eyes, enlarged in fear. But still she stands her ground, won't let him push open the door.

The child doesn't seem to be close by. Might've run to the back of the house to hide, frightened by raised voices. Doesn't she recognize Daddy's voice?

Dominique is telling him that Nicola is "expected back" by eight o'clock, which is virtually right now. Slight tremor in her voice, as if (just maybe) she isn't telling the truth.

Moving slowly, deliberately, not wanting to alarm the woman, though yes, wanting to scare the shit out of her, he reaches into his pocket, removes the lightweight barrette wrapped in pink tissue paper.

"Well. If you won't let me see my own daughter, maybe you can give this to her? See, it's a little—barrette—I think it's called."

Dominique takes the barrette from his fingers. Strained smile, trying to be polite, but not wanting to give him an inch nonetheless. Rapidly his eyes have moved over her. She is a good-looking woman even if pitch-black-skinned, muscled shoulders, legs, chest like protruding rocks, must be wearing some kind of thick-fiber sports bra beneath her shirt. Wide nose, nostrils. Damp-looking mouth. Wide hips. Smell of something musky, yeasty. Can't help himself, he feels a stab of sexual desire, resentment.

"Hey, Dominique? Just let me talk to my daughter for five minutes, okay? See, I missed her birthday . . ."

"Nicola told me not even to open the door if you showed up. So I got to close the door."

Taking the barrette from him, trying now to close the door in his face! Goddamn.

He makes a move to push past the woman who's blocking the way into his own house, but she's too fast for him, palm of her hand flat against his chest, pushing. And, in that instant, screaming bloody murder like a female on TV who is being attacked and wants the neighborhood to know.

Happens so fast, he can't process it.

His reactions are slow now. Slowed. Has to blink a dozen times to get his vision clear.

And why is the black woman screaming? Nobody touched her.

He's turning the doorknob of the (shut) door, rattling the door. He'd like to shake it open. Shake it off its hinges. But unless he breaks a window, he can't get in.

"Goddamned black cunt . . ."

Realizes now, he forgot the crowbar. Right beside the front steps in the bushes, he'd forgotten.

Could've thrust the crowbar through the door opening, used it to push the woman away. Once he got inside, use the crowbar to quiet her.

But it all happened too fast. As in combat, whatever happens, it happens without your volition, without your knowing what it is, when it begins, and when it is over, if it is over. And without your knowing (sometimes) if you are alive or—the opposite of alive . . .

He is furious. Humiliated. (Is the woman still screaming inside?)

Better escape now, before Nicola arrives. He has fucked up, but not totally.

Totally would be if he'd cracked the woman's skull. And then Nicola arrives, and he turns and cracks *hers*.

Almost for a moment Lew thinks that this has happened. He has had a glimpse of the fallen, broken female bodies at his feet.

Standing there in a daze while the black woman is (probably) calling Nicola. Or calling 911.

He is furious, shamed. Cheated of his little girl, which is his sole purpose in coming here.

Backs off, clenching and unclenching his stiff fingers. Have to know when to retreat. Intends to run to the Ford Warrior and escape but somehow finds himself making his way along the side of the house again, tapping on windows like some poor blind bastard.

"Meer-me? Sweetie? It's me—Daddy . . ."

He's outside the child's room. He thinks. Should be this window. Taps on it, a sharp staccato. And the miracle is, the venetian blind is being moved, lifted back. And there his daughter stands on the other side of the glass, only a few inches away, staring at him in awe. Fingers in her mouth.

Daddy is very excited. Daddy is thrilled.

"Hey sweetheart! Daddy loves you so, honey . . ."

Kisses the windowpane, clumsily. Smear of his mouth. Fool for love. He's high, he's risking everything, doesn't want to leave the premises without his precious little darling, but can't stay. He knows they are calling the police on him—the women.

Knows also, he has not broken any laws. He is sure. He did not (actually) force himself into the house. (And he is a co-owner!) He may have (accidentally) touched the black woman, but he did not hit her or harm her, though he was provoked. His word against hers.

Backs away. The child is pressed against the windowpane, small, perfect face obscured in shadow. But he knows she is gazing after him with a look of childish anguish, yearning.

If they were closer, and no barrier between them, he'd grab her in his arms. Lift her, bear her away with him forever.

Last thing he sees before turning to run to his vehicle is the little girl lifting her hand to wave.

Almost can hear the breathy voice—*Bye Daddy! I love you.*

Testimony

Don't ask. Don't make me see her.

She is gone, she has been missing for fifteen years. For most of my life.

I have learned to live without her . . .

When we married, I knew it was wrong—I knew that I did not deserve happiness with you.

I don't believe that there is Heaven, as you do. But there is Hell.

The Suicide

When you reciev this my brains will be blownout.
Will that make you happy, Nicola?
I am doing it for you, Nicola. To make you happy.

L.

Angry-scrawled in blue ballpoint on the reverse of a Crayola-bright postcard of the Rocky Mountains, Wyoming. Her eyes take in the words, her brain resists comprehending.

Who'd sent this? *Who?*

Then, the shock of what she has read sweeps over her. She is light-headed, reeling. Hears her fingernails scrape down the kitchen wall and finds herself sitting, hard.

Sinking onto a chair. Panting.

"No. Oh, no. No . . ."

She rereads the words. Stares at the photograph of mountains, scrubland, vivid-blue sky ribbed with clouds—colors too bright, pretty. The card slips from her trembling fingers, falls to the floor at her (bare, chilled) feet.

She is stunned. Disbelieving. Yet—it is unmistakably Lew's handwriting, and it is unmistakably Lew's voice.

More than once he'd threatened to kill himself.

Since before the separation. Many times after the divorce.

Himself, and her. And (possibly, unforgivably) the child.

We're all so unhappy, better for us to die together.

Just give a sign, Nicola.

I'll be waiting.

A sign! She'd had no idea what he meant.

He'd left Chautauqua Falls at least three months before. After he'd tried to force his way into the house, to see their daughter. Nicola had been at the community college at the time, teaching an evening class; her friend Dominique had been watching Miriam. Dominique called 911 but Lew had disappeared.

Next day, Nicola discovered a crowbar in the bushes beside the front door.

She'd been terrified that Lew would return. Though she'd spoken with police officers several times they didn't appear to take her very seriously; she had the idea that they knew Lew, or Lew knew them, in some capacity that excluded her. She was the complaining (ex)-wife, the hysterical (ex)-wife, unreliable and irrelevant.

Invariably she was asked if Lew had struck her, or their child. Had he been violent and smashed things, was he an alcoholic, did he use drugs, did he stalk her, did he threaten to kill her, what specifically had he *done?*

Yet it never seemed to matter, whatever she told them. How many times she told them. Until Lew actually injured her, or their daughter, or destroyed property in a way that constituted a crime, or involved others in his threats, the police did nothing.

After finding the crowbar in the bushes Nicola fled with Miriam to stay with friends for several days, elsewhere in Chautauqua Falls. She petitioned to family court to be granted an injunction against her ex-husband, to forbid him approaching her or Miriam or attempting in any way to make contact apart from his visitation rights with Miriam. But by then, Nicola had reason to believe that he'd left Chautauqua Falls.

He'd threatened to leave, many times. Disappear from her life. As if expecting Nicola to relent, and beg him to stay.

And possibly she did, at first. When it wasn't (yet) clear to her that a relationship with Lew Hayman was not in her best interest or in the best interest of their daughter.

From mutual friends, relatives, persons Nicola scarcely knew she'd heard that Lew had left Chautauqua Falls and was living "out west."

Reproachfully they addressed her, the (ex)-wife. The bitch of an (ex)-wife. For obviously *she* was to blame for the divorce and for Lew's deep misery.

All of them, on Lew's side. Why? Nicola was made to feel vicious, selfish.

At the start of their relationship Nicola had been very young. Lew was several years older, infinitely more experienced. Virtually against her wishes, he'd become her lover, before she was ready for so intense and physical a relationship, at seventeen. But soon, she'd come to love him helplessly . . . *Could be, you are my handmaid. Like the Bible says.*

He'd been joking. Of course.

She is staring at the lurid-bright postcard in her fingers. Mountains too dramatically russet red, sky too blue. Indeed, it is postmarked Laramie, Wyoming. September 17, 2006.

Nicola wonders, shivering—is this the *death date?*

She gropes for her cell phone on a counter nearby. Clumsy, stiff fingers eking out Lew's number, or what she recalls is Lew's number. But no—no longer.

Possibly he has a new cell phone. New number. New identity.

Possibly he'd destroyed his cell phone. Prior to killing himself.

Should she call 911? *Help is needed . . .*

But what could she tell the dispatcher? How to report a (possible) suicide in Laramie, Wyoming? Several days ago?

Nicola has no reason to think that Lew is even

in Laramie, or was. Just long enough to mail the postcard. Days have passed.

If he'd killed himself, it would be like him to have done it in a remote place. Forever then he would be *missing,* a *mystery.*

Nicola's mouth has gone dry. Thoughts rush at her; she cannot quite think.

It does not seem real to her, that Lew is dead. That Lew might be dead.

She feels a wave of guilt, nausea. If he has killed himself, she is to blame. In these very words, he has blamed her . . .

. . . *doing it for you, Nicola. To make you happy.*

He has cursed her! She will never outlive it.

Others will know. Miriam will know.

It would be like Lew to send postcards to a number of people. To make of his very suicide a scandal. There would be no way of shielding Miriam from the knowledge. So long as they live in Chautauqua Falls, where everyone knows everyone else and their lives are knitted together as by a multitude of spiderwebs overlapping.

A curse on her, and on their daughter as well . . .

She hates him! Goddamn his soul to Hell.

But she is crying. Hoarse, helpless sobs. Choking with grief. Horror and grief. Fury and grief. He did this to spite her—of course.

To come between her and the daughter, to ruin their lives.

Soon Miriam will be awake. It is still early,

not yet seven a.m. A pale, pearlescent sky of no weather, no wind. As if a great breath is being withheld.

Nicola has not dressed, she is in her cotton nightgown, barefoot. She'd come out into the kitchen to prepare coffee for herself. Shortly, she will prepare breakfast for Miriam and for herself, if she can eat. A very long day ahead. A day like a ladder that must be climbed step by step.

Stunning to realize how ignorant she'd been just a few minutes earlier. No idea what was awaiting her in the mailbox beside the door amid the usual flyers and bills. How naive, her feeling of well-being, of hope. For it's a teaching day, and Nicola prizes her teaching days. She is not (yet) a member of the permanent faculty at Chautauqua Falls Community College, but she has been told by her department chair that she will be eligible for tenure in another year. She teaches four composition classes of thirty students each, and they require hours of preparation, grading daily.

Each day a ladder. Steps she is eager, grateful to climb.

She has managed to sleep reasonably well recently. Sleep has been difficult for her, a torment. But since the divorce, and since Lew is no longer living in Chautauqua Falls, she is learning to sleep again, by degrees.

Learning to trust herself to fully undress again,

wear a nightgown to bed as a normal woman might do.

Nakedness is a luxury. The confidence required in making yourself vulnerable. Taking for granted that in the night you will not leap from your bed, fight off an assailant, run outside, run into the street crying for help . . . Exquisite luxury of *bare feet*.

Many times since he'd had to move out of the house Lew had teased, taunted. Maybe he'd drop by. Try the door? If the door is unlocked, he'd know he was welcome back.

Just give a sign, Nicola.

Never knew what that meant. Lew had always spoken mysteriously, cryptically. His speech was riddled with obscure allusions to heavy metal bands, video games. He'd never been religious, but he'd been, in his half-serious way, superstitious.

Waiting for a sign, Nicola. From you.

She'd been terrified that unknowingly, unconsciously she might *signal* him. She knew that he watched her, stalked her, seemed to be aware of her activities though (usually) she wasn't aware of his presence. Anxious about being alone in a parking lot, for instance. Wary of driving any distance alone if there wasn't much traffic. Walking by herself at night.

He'd been involved with other women, and lied about it, for years. Yet, separated from Nicola, he seemed to become more possessive of her, more insistent upon maintaining the marriage. He hadn't cared for the others, he told her. Only her.

You and Meer-me. My girls.

He'd been furious when Nicola declined to take him back. So long he'd been dominant in their relationship—Nicola the younger, weaker, less assertive—he'd taken for granted that when he asked to be forgiven, it was his wife's duty to forgive him.

Every woman he knew, he'd claimed, had dealt with her husband's infidelity from time to time. Every woman he knew had understood, forgiven, moved on.

But no, Nicola decided. Not this time.

She had a job; she could support herself and Miriam. She wasn't financially dependent on him any longer, as she'd been years ago.

She was no longer a child. A girl. She was a woman, and a mother. Her duty was to protect Miriam and herself.

They began to quarrel violently. For Nicola no longer shrank away in shock or in hurt; she was no longer hesitant to speak back to Lew, to scream at him when he interrupted her, as he did constantly.

Finally, he moved out. For a while he lived with a woman friend, as a gesture of defiance to Nicola.

Essentially, he could not believe that Nicola no longer adored him without qualification. That she was serious about a separation, and eventually a divorce.

He'd begun drinking heavily. He had medical issues. He was in debt. He quarreled with employers, walked off the job.

He didn't exactly make verbal threats against Nicola, nothing that repeated (or recorded) was likely to impress law enforcement officers as constituting grounds for an arrest or a reprimand. Words that issued from his mouth often seemed as surprising to him as they were to her. You'd think—*Is he joking?* Many times she'd laughed, uneasy—*What did he just say? He can't be serious.*

Before even he'd enlisted in the U.S. Army, he'd said outrageous things. But there he'd culti-vated a cruel use of seemingly ordinary speech, given a mock-Southern inflection. Like a butter knife honed razor-sharp.

Never anything she might have recorded to play for skeptical police officers. No.

But with Dominique as a witness, a vehement and convincing witness, Nicola had succeeded in getting an injunction against Lew. For whatever good an injunction might do.

The family court judge to whom Nicola and her attorney appealed had seemed sympathetic with her, genuinely concerned. The crowbar in the bushes made a strong impression, as well as Dominique's description of Lew's "rage." Unsurprisingly, the judge was a woman.

Lew was behind in child payments, several months. Nicola has given up expecting him to pay. In gratitude for his staying away from them, she has been unwilling to complain.

No alimony. Nicola had known better than to press for alimony.

Wondering now: Should she call Lew's mother? His family?

If he has killed himself, they should know. Or perhaps they already knew.

Since the separation Nicola has been estranged from the Haymans. If they see her, they turn away in disgust, indignation. Once, Lew's mother had liked Nicola very much, like a favorite daughter—now, she seemed to despise her.

It wasn't just the separation and divorce that had turned them against her. Nicola discovered that Lew had maligned her as a slut, a whore.

He'd told anyone who would listen, and there were many of these, that she'd had an affair, affairs. That she drank, took drugs. That she was a negligent mother.

Male colleagues with whom she'd been friendly began to avoid her, not wanting to be included in Lew's wild accusations. Mutual friends were embarrassed for her, and of her. Even as Lew assured her that he loved her, couldn't live without her, he was telling sordid lies about her, as she would discover to her chagrin.

She knew how he lied about her, yet there was little she could do about it. Lies, so often repeated, metastasized through the dense, overlapping spiderwebs of Chautauqua Falls.

He'd sabotaged even their early years together. Claiming it was Nicola, and not Lew, who'd wanted an abortion when Nicola was pregnant with Miriam. Claiming that Nicola had in fact had two or three abortions before they were married.

None of this was remotely true. Lew had enlisted in the army to avoid Nicola's pregnancy. He hated squalling babies and diapers, he said. Later he would claim how much he loved his beautiful little daughter as soon as he'd set eyes on her.

It was true. Or true in some way. That he loved Miriam, and he loved Nicola. But at the same time, Nicola thought, he'd wanted to hurt them. If he couldn't live with them and be Daddy, he wanted to hurt them badly.

And so, he has killed himself. To take revenge.

She'd fantasized Lew killing himself, Nicola has to admit. Driving his car off the road, drunk. Drunk and despairing. An overdose of opioids. He'd returned from Iraq with a wounded body. His short-term memory was impaired. His peripheral vision was impaired. Technically, he should not have been driving. He should not have been allowed to own a gun.

In his jokey way he'd imagined his death. Hanging. Gun. Suicide-by-cop. Car-crash-on-Thruway. Not funny, Nicola pleaded, but he'd only laughed and told her to lighten up.

He knew a dozen Iraq War vets who'd killed themselves. It was generally known, there was an epidemic of suicide among former soldiers. Men he'd befriended at the VA hospital when he'd been there. An uncle of his, a veteran of the Gulf War, had killed himself years ago with a twelve-gauge shotgun in the backyard of his home, his wife less than twelve feet away.

Lew did own a gun, she knew. He'd won it in a poker game. And rifles he'd owned as a kid on the farm in Shaheen, inherited from his older brothers. The handgun, a revolver, he'd had trouble getting a license to carry concealed on his person, since New York State has strict gun control laws. Nicola isn't sure if in fact Lew had ever gotten a license in New York State, but if he'd moved to Wyoming owning a handgun, any sort of gun, carrying it concealed anywhere he wanted would not have been a problem.

Gun suicides were frequent in Wyoming, Nicola had read. Twice the rate of most other states. Almost exclusively men.

Uneasily she wonders if Lew had his gun when he tried to force his way into the house.

She wonders if he'd meant to kidnap Miriam. He might have shot Dominique!—might have murdered her with the crowbar. Nicola has no idea if he'd returned to the house while she and Miriam were staying with friends, but she does know that Chautauqua Falls police officers have a warrant for his arrest, following Dominique's complaint, which they've never been able to serve.

Has he ever abused your daughter? Nicola's fierce-intelligent (female) lawyer asked.

And Nicola could not reply *I think so, yes.*

For it is unjust, even in speaking of a brutal man, to preface *yes* with *I think.*

Nicola has not wished to think about her (ex)-husband and their daughter. What Lew may have done with and to their daughter. She has not wished to ask Miriam, even circumspectly. She is fearful of knowing, but she is more fearful of the prospect of traumatizing the little girl by asking questions that will upset her.

Daddy's custody days were Saturday (pickup no earlier than nine a.m.) and Sunday (return no later than six p.m.). Once weekly, but after the injunction reduced to alternate weekends.

After a weekend with Daddy, Miriam was often excited and fretful and rebellious about going to bed at her usual hour. Her fine, fair-brown hair was matted and snarled. Her shoelaces were knotted. She was famished, but not for the food her mother prepared. Once, Miriam was brought back home on Sunday evening with her little shirt crookedly buttoned.

None of this meant anything, Nicola thought. Though it could be made to mean something, she could not bring herself to go on the offensive against the child's father.

It was crucial to Nicola that Miriam did not seem to fear her father.

Indeed, Miriam looked forward to weekends with Daddy and was anxious and disappointed when, as sometimes happened, Daddy failed to show up.

Nicola stood at a window with the little girl, gazing out. Annoyed with Lew when he disappointed Miriam, though relieved, obviously. Thinking—*This person you call Daddy is not coming for you. This morning or ever. He never loved you or your mother. Let him step off the face of the earth. God, thank you!*

Of course it was exactly like Lew to fail to show up for visits with his daughter after he'd fought bitterly for these visits. It was the spirit of the custody, not its literal application, that concerned him.

His dignity. His rights. The daughter was *his right*.

But you don't always need to exercise your rights. Lew insisted.

Well, Nicola has exercised certain rights of her

145

own. A formal—legal—"separation." Removing her wedding ring, at last—too loose on her finger anyway.

Replacing the wedding band with a delicate silver ring, a small cloudy-blue opal that she'd had as a girl, passed on to her by her grandmother, who'd worn it as a girl.

One day, she will pass the ring on to Meer-me. Comforting to think so, though also sad.

Bittersweet, that sensation. Sweetbitter.

What a relief to be free of him these past three months!—the dreaded husband. Yet she has missed him, too. Even the threat of him. She has missed the touch of his hot skin, the urgency of his desire. His (possessive) eyes on her, seeing her as she could never see herself.

The unpredictability of the man, she had to concede. Unlike other men who are predictable, safe.

He'd rarely spoken of Iraq. You could not ask him a direct question. *(Hey, you kiddin'? You don't want to know.)* But in a quieter mood, alone with Nicola and feeling reasonably good about himself, he might speak to her in a less defensive way, as if thinking aloud.

In a combat zone, he said, if there was an attack, when you didn't know if you'd be alive in five minutes, the barrier between the present and the future becomes very thin. Almost, you can peer through it, as if you are looking through a curtain—not that you see what is actually coming at you but you see its shape, its dimensions.

But can you change it? Nicola asked.

No. You can't change it, Lew said. *Only get out of the fucking way so that it happens to someone else.*

Barefoot, like Mommy, on the chilly linoleum floor, the child hovers in the doorway, uncertain.

Is Mommy crying? Why is Mommy crying?

It is very frightening to see Mommy cry, tears shining on her cheeks. To see any adult cry.

Worse, to see that Mommy sees her and is not trying to hide her face.

Nicola denies that she is crying. Nicola rubs at her reddened eyes, which itch badly, and so it is, Nicola's eyes are shiny but dry.

"Mommy is not crying, silly. Mommy is happy."

Nicola goes to Miriam, stooping to gather the shivering child in her arms. Saying, with a kiss, since Miriam is looking doubtful, her flannel pajama top falling over one small shoulder, "Mommy is *very happy.*"

Testimony

Yes, but I heard her crying. When she thought I was asleep. Hiding her face in a pillow, crying. And the pillow sodden-wet afterward, well into the next day.

Heard her on the phone. For days. I could not count the days. Her hoarse, lowered voice, then silence. The silence of rebuke, of chagrin. Silence of shame.

Whoever she spoke with, of my (lost) father. For I would hear his name whispered—Lew.

They were accusing her, I knew. Sometimes she refuted them—No! Goddamn no, I did not. *But more often she assented, in silence.*

His family, his mother. Family court officers, police officers, her lawyer. A New York State police detective, with whom a friend had put her in contact, who could speak with Laramie, Wyoming, law enforcement.

Was my father dead? Deceased?

Without a body, could there be a death certificate?

Nothing online. Nothing she could find, though she searched obsessively, day after day and many times a day.

Obituaries. Scrolling through obituaries. Hayman, Hayward, Handeman, Herman. John Doe.

Wyoming, Montana, Utah, Colorado, Nevada.

But would there be an obituary for an unknown person? For mere remains? A skeleton? Where would such an obituary appear? For it seemed likely that my father had taken his own life in a remote place in the Rocky Mountains. On the high plain. Out of spite, fury. Out of self-loathing, that he no longer had a family. Vultures would strip his bones. His clothes would fall from the air in tatters as the great birds beat their wings rising. His mangled hiking boots would be left behind.

What could I have done differently?—my mother asks.

Bitter, incredulous. Speaking on the phone or to herself. Not seeming to care that I could overhear, even if I pressed my hands against my ears.

Nothing! Nothing I could have done differently.

Oh God. I loved him so much.

And now I see her face: pale skin, a very thin skin, pale freckles, hazel eyes widened in bewilderment, hurt. It is a young face for my mother is (still) a young woman, fifteen years ago in the final year of her life.

Looking toward me, but not seeing me. Though I can see her, Mommy can't see me, why is that?

"Crime Scene"

On TV it would be a crime scene. In the house on Grant Street, when Miriam returned from school, it was just Mommy's bedroom.

If you knew where to look, you would see the rupture. This is a word that comes to her many years later—*rupture.*

"Mommy?"—The child's voice is thin, hesitant.

The (big) bed has been made, for Mommy always makes her bed as soon as she gets up in the morning, unless it's a day to change bedclothes, which is once a week, usually Saturday, in which case she will not make the bed immediately after getting up, but later in the morning after doing the laundry.

Sometimes Miriam helps Mommy make the (big) bed. Mommy on one side of the bed and Miriam on the other. Each lifting the cotton coverlet and giving it a shake upward so it billows a little, like a balloon settling.

Looking across the bed, there's Mommy, smiling at her.

Shaking the pillows into fresh pillowcases. Some pillows fit into cases more tightly than others and require emphatic shaking. Then, pushing your hand deep inside the pillowcase to tug the corners of the pillow into the corners of the pillowcase, which is tricky.

Mommy says, Not quite, sweetie. Keep trying.

It is not much fun to make a bed alone. It is always fun to make a bed with Mommy.

Not once in her life, in all the years remaining, will she make a bed, fluff up sheets, force pillows into tight pillowcases, and not think of her mother, Nicola, smiling at her across the expanse of a bed.

In this case, it is a weekday, not laundry day.

The (big) bed has been made as usual, but it is in disarray now. There is disorder here. Something has happened. The bedclothes have been tugged out of place. Sharp creases in the rose-colored coverlet, as if someone grabbed at it as she was being pulled away.

A lampshade is askew. Venetian blinds are crooked. Bureau drawers have been pulled out.

A book from the public library that Mommy has been reading, on the floor where she would never have left it. *American Women's Poetry from Anne Bradstreet to Adrienne Rich* spread-eagled on the floor.

Inside this book are several sheets of paper, computer printouts of maps of Wyoming, one of them annotated in red ink—circles drawn around the small city of Laramie and the small towns Granite Springs and Herenden, a dotted red line connecting Laramie and the interstate highway.

It will not be determined where the maps were printed as Nicola's home computer isn't attached to a printer, but it will be speculated that she'd used a printer at the community college.

It is 3:25 p.m., October 14, 2006. This will be the last day Miriam sleeps in the house on Grant Street—either in the (big) bed with Mommy or in her own child-size bed in the adjacent room.

She is a big girl now, six years old and in first grade.

She is not a big girl. She will never remember a day of first grade.

Feeling the hairs stir at the nape of her neck, seeing another wrong thing—Mommy's closet door flung open.

There is an agitation of the air that makes breathing increasingly difficult.

Miriam has just returned home. Run into the house. *Mommy? Mom-my?* Excited, elated.

But now there are these wrong things. Her eyes dart rapidly about, seeing and not seeing.

A minute earlier, Mrs. Neeley had let Miriam out of her car at the foot of the driveway. Mrs. Neeley is Barbara's mother, and Barbara Neeley is Miriam's best friend at DeWitt Clinton Elementary.

Though the school is only three blocks away, a five-minute walk, Nicola's mother doesn't think it is a good idea for Miriam to walk to and from school just yet. Next year, maybe. Or the next.

Yes, other children in the neighborhood walk. Older children walk.

But not Miriam, not just yet.

"Mommy?"

Miriam examines some of the things scattered on the floor by the bureau. She is beginning to pant, a frightened little animal.

It will be discovered that numerous items are missing from the household. Nicola's sister-in-law Traci Hayman will aid police officers in the inventory.

Nicola's purse (wallet, credit cards, cash), checkbook, cell phone. Judging from empty hangers in the closet, several articles of clothing. Possibly two or three pairs of shoes. Underwear, socks.

Suitcase! Traci sees that Nicola's suitcase is missing.

No car in the driveway or in the garage. Car missing.

You know what I think?—She couldn't stand it. Not knowing.

Had to go there. See if she could find him.

. . . find the remains?

Find him. He's alive. For sure, Lew Hayman is not dead.

But wouldn't she have told us? Anyone?

Wouldn't have left their daughter behind. Never.

Wouldn't have left without telling anyone. Unless—

—unless she did, and the note got lost. Email got lost.

What might've happened—he contacted her. Called her.

Her hair was falling out, you could see—thinning.

Driving all that way?—alone?

People do desperate things. We can't judge.

And so they ask Miriam: Did your mother tell you she was going away? Did she say where she was going? Did she say when she was coming back? Did she say she would come back to you?

Miriam nods her head, *yes.*

So ashamed that Mommy has gone away and left her! Hears herself say in a whisper, *yes.*

Reconnoiter, Surveillance, Attack, Mission Accomplished

By the world's reckoning, he has been dead for twenty-seven days.

He has established his death date for the record, sending postcards to selected individuals responsible for it: September 17, 2006.

The mission has been carefully planned. Not a step in the mission has been left to chance or improvisation.

No one knows his name any longer. His name is listed (he believes) among the dead.

Like a penitent—indeed, he *is* a penitent—he has shaved his head. Coarse dark-brown hair laced with gray, receding from his forehead—very deliberately he has cut this hair. He has shaved his (scarred, discolored) scalp, hiding the ugly reddened patches of skin beneath a white cotton cap with red-stitched letters SHERWIN-WILLIAMS PAINTS.

Shaved his head, also his eyebrows. But has allowed his (coarse, gray-grizzled) whiskers to sprout halfway down his chest, like an Old Testament prophet.

Clothes he wears now—paint-splotched denim jacket hiding scarred arms; paint-splotched work pants with numerous pockets, nothing like anything he'd worn when he'd lived in Chautauqua Falls. But he will never give up his old hiking boots, not until they rot from his feet.

Leather-band digital wristwatch, appropriated from an individual who had no use for it any longer. Black nylon backpack, found discarded in a Greyhound bus station in Stanton, Colorado.

The wronged husband has returned to New York State by bus. A pilgrimage of many days.

Days of open vistas, endless skies. High desert. Flat plains. Plenty of time to turn his thoughts over and over like turning over earth with a shovel.

The woman and the girl—*his*.

Why should a man surrender his possessions? He should not, and will not.

At least, the woman. The woman is the betrayer. The child, an innocent bystander—"collateral damage."

Tries to recollect the child but is distracted by thoughts of the woman—*wife*.

As the wronged husband, he will give her the opportunity to repent. To express remorse. He is generous enough to forgive. He has forgiven many who have not deserved forgiveness.

In sickness and in health. Till death do us part. What is yours is mine.

What is mine is yours.

In Chautauqua Falls he makes his way on foot from the bus terminal downtown to his destination (Grant Street) two miles away. It is a mild, damp day. He soon begins to perspire, for the air is humid. He walks with a slight limp, it is shameful to him. His legs ache, knees ache. Shrapnel fragments in his legs. Could be shrapnel fragments making their way to his heart like blood clots. He does not walk fast, but he walks steadily. He will not be deterred. He will not be cheated of justice.

At the edges of his vision there is mist, fog— it is startling to him when objects (vehicles, people) emerge abruptly into the center of his vision, nearly upon him. He has learned not to reveal surprise when this happens, but to remain calm and in control, and this is why, though he carries a (loaded) .44-caliber revolver with him at all times, the weapon is safely in his backpack and not on his person. He cannot reach it readily and discharge it.

One breath at a time!

This town in which, all the years of his adult life he'd lived here, he'd driven a vehicle. Walking in Chautauqua Falls is an exercise in humility that (he concedes) is good for him.

In work clothes splotched with paint, a man is invisible.

Paint splotches, painter's cap—camouflage.

If he sights someone he knows or believes he knows, a familiar or almost-familiar face, he will proceed as if in ignorance, unaware. Secure in the knowledge that the other will not see *him.*

Side streets, back alleys. Pearce Avenue, where there is no sidewalk, only a narrow shoulder for pedestrians. Yet soon he arrives at Grant Street.

On foot. For it is the woman's vehicle they will be taking.

Surveillance on Grant for as many hours as required.

The previous time, when he'd knocked on the door, forthright, a fool. Allowing the glaring black female to ID him.

A blunder. Mistake. Could've been tackled by police in his own driveway, thrown onto his face. Choke hold, cuffs. He has been arrested, he knows the sickening sensation of a man's knee in the small of the back, pinning you down in triumph. Daring you to resist, fight for your life.

He has been tased. He has been beaten, humbled. He has considered exposing himself to enemy fire and making an end of his fucked-up life. He has considered dousing himself with gasoline and immolating himself in the smelly front foyer of the VA hospital in Buffalo. On the steps of Chautauqua Falls Family Court, making of himself a martyr to all wronged husbands, betrayed fathers.

He has considered slashing his wrist with the hunting knife. The carotid artery in his neck rawly spurting blood onto the woman's guilty face.

But no: not yet. It is not that time, yet.

Here is a surprise: her car is in the driveway . . . In the late morning, the woman is home.

Not teaching? (Has her husband's death so devastated Nicola that she has taken a leave from the community college?)

(Feels a stab of tenderness for the woman. Mounting excitement.)

Another man would be rocked back on his heels. Such good luck!

He isn't surprised. The prepared man makes his own goddamned luck.

Slips on his gloves—frayed leather gloves with tight fingers.

Approaches the house. Not the front door (likely to be locked), but the side door by the garage (likely to be unlocked). Turns the doorknob, enters like a man returning to his home.

Swiftly then, and silently, not giving the woman the opportunity to discover him.

Through the kitchen, into the hall, headed for the bedroom—*his* bedroom—enters on the run—limping, but fast—not giving the faithless wife a chance to scream, even as, her back to the doorway, seeing his reflection in a mirror she is facing, she turns to him with an expression of utter astonishment.

Immediately he is on her. Has her from behind as she tries to flee. Forearm clamped across her throat, hand over her mouth, pressed tight.

She is struggling, panicked. Eyes widened in terror.

Tries to claw his face, kick at him. He grips her tighter. In an instant he could break her neck, she knows that, doesn't she?

Hey! He laughs at her. What's she think, this is some kind of fucking game?

In a calmer voice, he assures her he is not going to hurt her. Not as she has hurt him.

He wants (only) to talk to her, he says. As she had not allowed him to talk to her when he'd been alive.

Laughs, for this is funny. When he'd rehearsed on the Greyhound bus, he laughed aloud too, imagining the look on the woman's face he is seeing now.

Only yourself to blame, Nicola. Gravely he intones.

Would've made all the difference, he says, if she'd only allowed him to return to this house, to sit down with her, to break bread with her like man and wife. Man and wife and *child*.

She'd disrespected him. Betrayed him. Went outside the marriage.

She'd hired a lawyer. Told vicious lies about him in family court. Took his daughter from him. Cost him his reputation, his job, and his life.

Repeats, he will not hurt her if she doesn't scream. If she will just talk to him. If he releases her . . .

He is hurting her, he knows. Very close to breaking her neck.

So easily that might be done. His hands, in the tight-fingered gloves, clench tight. If she struggles, the hands are further aroused.

Nicola has tried to wrench free of his grip, but she is not strong enough. Tries to claw at his arm, her nails breaking against the denim sleeve. Weak-kneed with terror, she would sink to the floor, but he holds her up.

Nicola!—he speaks sternly.

Has to laugh, how surprised she is. Maybe, at first, she hadn't even known who it was—crease-faced, leathery-skinned from spending time outdoors, eyebrows shaved, grizzled-gray whiskers halfway down his chest.

"See?—it's me, your husband. Risen from the grave."

Of course she knows him now. Knows his smell as he knows hers.

Promising her again: he won't hurt her if she doesn't scream.

Won't hurt her if she doesn't try to get away.

Nicola is struggling just to breathe. Not his plan, to smother her.

Wants her *alive.* For as long as there is hope.

Cautiously he draws the gloved hand away from her mouth. Broken, defeated, the faithless wife indicates *yes.*

Her voice is gone. She is gasping for breath.

Her skin is dead white. He can smell the panic on her skin.

It is not generally known, he tells her. How quick a human being can become a panicked animal.

In a combat zone, you see that all the time. You smell yourself, strongest. Ain't pretty.

It seems that Nicola is not going to scream. She understands the futility of screaming. The neighbors would probably not hear, and this time of day, neighbors might not be at home. She is (evidently) alone in the house, the child is at school. And so she is not fearful of the child being hurt. She is fearful for herself, but not the child. That must be some consolation for her, the mother. This he understands.

Gently informing her: if she cooperates, they will not be here when Meer-me comes home.

When Meer-me comes home, they will be gone.

Meer-me will be allowed to stay behind, for now.

"If you cooperate. If you don't scream. If you follow my instructions. If you come with me."

Nicola is dazed, uncertain. But she can breathe now, the yearning to live has flooded her body.

The yearning to protect the child possesses her.

And so she acquiesces. Agreeing to cooperate without knowing what it will mean, only that the child will be spared.

She is only partly dressed; she has been preparing to go out. (To her beloved college, he supposes.) Brusquely he tells her to finish dressing, put on shoes. Pack.

Pack?—Nicola stares at him.

(What does she see, he wonders. Righteous, glaring eyes, bristling whiskers. Somewhere deep inside is the swaggering, good-looking young man she'd once adored and had not yet learned to fear.)

From the closet he removes her suitcase, knows exactly where it's kept, shoved into a corner. Tosses it onto the bed. Tells her to pack what she needs for a few days, hurry, no time to waste, he will lose patience.

"We're going on a retreat. Second honeymoon."

Laughs at her, cringing before him. Forlorn, wondering.

He knows what she is wondering—*Will he murder me? What will he do to me?*

It's true, the wronged husband has brought his eight-inch stainless steel hunting knife, which is, nonetheless, slightly stained. And he has brought his .44-caliber revolver, won in a poker game, fired only three times (so far). And a sizable length of twine and duct tape. And a pair of handcuffs, purchased in a pawnshop in Stanton, Colorado.

All these items, and others, in the black nylon backpack.

However, it isn't part of his essential plan to use any of these. These are backups if his mission fails.

Final solution—the default strategy.

"I told you, Nicola. Second honeymoon."

Though, in fact, they'd never had a first.

Stunned by the sight of him. She'd believed him dead.

A roaring in her ears. She can barely hear his instructions.

Throwing clothes into the suitcase. He has yanked open bureau drawers, rummaged in the closet. Hurry!

Tosses shoes at her feet. She winces as a shoe strikes her bare foot.

Lew's old impatience in the household. Intimacy you can't revoke.

Once the man has entered the female body. Once he has taken possession, you risk your life denying him.

"Returning to claim my bride," he is saying.

"Returning from the dead, eh? Surprised you?"

He laughs, baring discolored teeth and a gap between lower front teeth she has never seen before.

Elation in his face; bloodshot glistening eyes. He is high, his skin shimmering with heat.

Favoring his left leg. Where he was wounded. Still, he is fast on his feet. Shocking to her, the ex-husband is not only alive but *livid*.

Yes, she knows it will (probably) be a mistake to leave the house with this man. To leave the house, which is safety.

Yet if she refuses to leave, he will hurt her. Badly.

He will wait, in hiding. He will wait for Miriam. What he will do with Miriam—to Miriam—she cannot allow herself to imagine.

So she will go with him. She is cooperating, packing. Trying to recall when she'd last packed this suitcase and where she'd gone, but she cannot.

Can she summon help? How?

Once in the car with him. Opening the door, throwing herself out . . .

With part of her mind desperate to believe when he repeats he will not hurt her if she cooperates.

Not going to hurt our daughter. Of all of us, she is the innocent one.

She understands, the ex-husband is very angry. He is trembling with rage. Yet he manages to speak calmly, as one might speak to a terrified child.

The coarse, matted whiskers are fascinating to her, repugnant. She feels a thrill of disgust—if he tries to kiss her . . .

Cannot remember when he'd last kissed her. Or she'd kissed him.

An angry, biting sort of "kiss"—mashing his mouth against hers, to subdue, hurt. Vaguely she recalls.

Wanting to inform him that she is expected at the college within the hour.

She has a meeting, she might inform him.

(In fact, she has only office hours, through the afternoon.) In the late afternoon she will teach one of her remedial composition courses— English as a Second Language.

Wanting to tell him that she will be missed, there will be a call to the house when she fails to arrive at the college.

Wanting to tell him he should leave immediately, and she will not report him . . .

At 3:15 her friend Dominique will pick Miriam up from school and will remain with her (in the house) until Nicola returns home at about seven p.m.

But that will be too late. By then, Lew will have taken her away, to wherever he has planned to take her.

Too late, too late! Dominique will enter this house hours too late.

But: Would she want Dominique and Miriam to walk in on them?—in this house? She does not. She fears for their safety.

Dominique had warned her: that man is capable of great harm.

That man is capable of great harm against his own family.

And so, better for Nicola to leave with him. Obey him. Throw herself on his mercy.

He is not a bad person, Nicola has often told herself. Bad things have happened to him, he has acted badly . . . But Lew is not a *bad person.*

We tell ourselves. An incantation.

He will threaten, he will rage. But he would not hurt me . . .

Assuring her it's just to talk. Talk things through. *Honeymoon. Amnesty.* As in the early days of their marriage, when they'd lain in bed talking into the early hours of the night.

(*He* talked, Nicola recalls. She listened.)

Out of his backpack Lew removes several sheets of printed paper. A map? Maps? Something he seems to have prepared for carefully. He inserts the sheets of paper in a library book that has been knocked to the floor beside Nicola's bed.

Panic grips her: Has he prepared her suicide note?

In the kitchen he instructs her: fill a grocery bag.

Food in the refrigerator, canned goods in the cupboard. Cheerios in the bright yellow box exactly where he recalls.

"Okay, we need a second bag." This one, Lew fills himself.

Fills several plastic containers with water. Enough to last for a several days if they are frugal.

In a bag, forks, knives. Can opener.

And now, walk beside him out of the house. As if nothing is wrong.

Carrying the grocery bags to the car in the driveway. Water bottles, suitcase.

Just a trip they are taking: a couple.

Husband, wife. Going away for a few days.

She hesitates. She is swaying on her feet. If she faints, she might save herself.

Nicola has fainted several times in her life. All but one of these times occurred within the past year, as the stress of her life has increased.

But not now. His hand grips her upper arm, tight.

With a hint of just how tight he might grip her, if he wishes.

His fingers have always been strong, willful.

Will of their own. Volition of their own.

Stiff-walking Nicola to the other side of the car. Passenger's seat.

Surprised, he notices that the air is very light outdoors. Sky like vapor. He fumbles for sunglasses in one of the deep khaki pockets. How bold the wronged husband is, how brazen, stepping outside where anyone might see him/them.

But no one observes. At this hour of the day, Grant Street is very quiet. Fate is on the side of the wronged husband.

He has her key. Key to the car. Knowing exactly where Nicola would keep her car keys, the little wooden bowl on a counter, he'd scooped it up.

A little bowl in which she/they keep coins, also. Many nickels, pennies.

He laughs harshly. Chiding the wife for the fact that the car in the driveway isn't a car he knows.

Isn't a car he has ever driven.

So where'd she get the car? (One of the men she's been screwing?)

Nicola stammers something about the car. Pre-owned, a bargain. Her old car had broken down. He isn't even listening. Gives her a shake to indicate that's enough.

In their marriage, the husband requires that the wife reply to his queries, remarks. The wife dare not retreat into silence. But, having indicated her readiness to speak, the wife need not speak at length.

She recalls that now. The first of their intimacies.

They are outside in the bright vaporous air. He could not have said what the season is fall or spring. Mild, cool air. Mists.

Breathing strangely. Oxygen is failing her brain. Calculating whether to scream or to run . . . But he is a veteran of the U.S. Army, he has served his country in combat. He knows exactly what is going through the woman's brain.

Make a run for it. Make a break. Try.

Actually he feels a measure of sympathy. The panicked doe will suddenly break free, run from her captor, except of course she cannot run from her captor, who has hold of her with such strength. If he wished, he could break her arm just above the elbow.

Chop of his hand, deft and furious, could break her slender neck.

Yes yes *yes*. He is her master, she will obey him.

Numbly she climbs into the car. *Her* car, but she will sit (meekly) in the passenger's seat.

He opens the trunk, tosses in the suitcase. He is panting, exhilarated. But is there something missing?

In the rehearsal, he has sometimes bound, gagged, placed the female in the trunk of the car. If she hadn't cooperated.

Stuff a rag in her mouth. Filthy mouth that has uttered such lies about him. Lied to him vowing love, honor, obey.

It is repulsive, the woman's mouth is beautiful, as the woman is beautiful (as he recalls). Her frightened eyes brimming with tears of apprehension, regret.

"Crouch down," he tells her. So no one can see her.

Just until they get out of town.

She crouches down. Hands on the nape of her neck, as if she is holding herself still, hiding her face.

(Is she crying? His heart is suffused with something like pity.)

(If she is crying, that means she is repentant. He is magnanimous, he can forgive.)

(But not too quickly! That would be a blunder.)

Drives along Pearce Avenue at the speed limit. Precisely.

If a cop stops him, the woman will scream for help.

If a cop stops him, he will not have easy access to the backpack (now in the back seat) where the .44-caliber revolver is hidden.

At the city line, Pearce becomes a state highway. On the state highway the speed limit is forty-five miles an hour, which he will also not exceed.

Home! He is returning *home.*

Bringing the woman, the faithless wife, to his first home.

Driving south and west into the foothills of the Chautauqua mountains. Country miles on twisting roads, where distances are misleading. He has memorized the route. He has driven this route countless times in his sleep. Sterling Lake, Round Pond. Snyder, Tinturn, Shaheen, Shaheen Junction. It has been years, he feels both dread and hope.

His skin is hot. Sunbaked. He has not slept for how many days and nights, open-eyed on the Greyhound bus, hurtling toward his destiny.

Home. Not that it was ever home. Remembers wanting to burn the goddamn barns down, toss a match into the hay. So sick of milking cows, the stench of cow shit, shoveling manure.

So sick of *home.* How strange then, he has no other home to return to.

Fields of corn and soybeans, desiccated now in October. So some farmland is still being cultivated.

Turning onto Carpenter Road, paved for a few miles. Then, unpaved.

Recalling how, when he was a kid, a stretch of Carpenter Road had sunk into a kind of ravine opening in the earth one morning after a heavy rainstorm. Beside the road, a creek of muddy, rushing water.

He tells Nicola this. This memory. *Act of God!*—people said.

Had to be an act of God, if God "acts" in our lives.

Actually, he has told Nicola this before. Nicola nods, recalling.

This bond between them: husband, wife. Can't just break it, hope to walk away.

You can barely see the creek running beside the road, so many trees and bushes have sprung up. What was once farmland is reverting to wilderness. Fewer people live in Shaheen than when he was a kid.

He says, feels like *forsaken* here. Peace and silence.

Except: the woman is weeping. Out of sheer nerves, the woman is weeping.

As if to console, the woman's hands clasp each other on her knees.

Is she realizing belatedly that she has lost her chance to escape?

When they'd been in Chautauqua Falls. When they'd been in traffic.

Now they are twelve miles south and west of town. Bumping along a rutted road. She has seen the old Hayman farm; she has even stayed here with Lew when Lew's mother was still alive and Lew's older sister, Traci, was living here, taking care of her. Years ago.

Some of this returns to her.

But could Nicola have escaped back on the highway? Throwing herself out of the passenger's door? Lew would have prevented it at once. Quick as a snake, Lew's hand that had often leaped toward her when they'd quarreled, feigning a blow.

He hadn't hit her, though. Not hard. Not often. Not really to hurt, rather to chastise. She'd told herself. At first.

Which is why she has agreed to cooperate now.

Also knowing there was no reasonable chance for escape. The man's fingers could so easily break her neck.

Since the U.S. Army, Iraq. Since the angry silence in him, of what was done to him there, and what he'd done.

Turning into the weed-choked driveway of the old farmhouse. Grim, weatherworn shingles, a rotted and sagging roof. In tall grasses at the front, a forlorn FOR SALE sign.

His mother's will is still in probate court, so far as Lew knows. It was poorly executed, many times revised. And there were debts, complications. Though Lew has been informed that Traci is the heir to the (severely diminished) estate, he understands that he too, as the son, is also an heir, for his mother would have left the property to him if he'd hung around, taken care of her in her old age, her illness, as Traci had. For sure! The old woman had always loved him best.

Carefully he drives the car along the rutted driveway to the rear of the house and beyond, through waves of grasses and thistles, into the dilapidated hay barn.

Parks the car there, as far from the (open) barn door as possible.

With some effort he will manage to slide that door shut. With the woman's assistance. So that no one on the road will see a vehicle inside. If anyone comes looking.

An alternate plan, devised on the Greyhound trip, is Round Pond.

Round Pond is not visible from any road and is unexpectedly deep—maybe ten feet.

There's a small hill above Round Pond, he remembers. Release the brake, the car would roll down the hill.

Water snakes in Round Pond, but maybe driving the vehicle in, letting the vehicle sink, would scare the fuckers away.

In Round Pond, the (compact) car would be submerged. The bottom is soft, muddy. Once the car sank, it would likely settle even deeper, in time.

But that is only if things go poorly between them. If the reconciliation fails. It is good to have Round Pond as a default. Gagged, wrists and ankles tied tight, the woman would fit snugly in the trunk of the car, if he removed the spare tire, and never be discovered.

(What to do with the spare tire? Could sink it into the pond with the car or keep for future use.)

(But whose future use? Squints, looking into the future, but can't make out the details.)

He could escape on foot. He still has money. He can return to Wyoming anytime he fucking wishes.

Or drive into the pond with the woman. Man and wife. One flesh.

Rehearsing on the Greyhound bus, he'd wakened to see a couple immolated together, frantic leaping flames.

Wondering how painful it would be. Fire. There'd been men burned alive in combat. Third-degree burns over ninety percent of the body. When pain is too powerful to be measured, the brain goes blank.

He has been standing motionless beside the car for—how long? Minutes? As the woman stares at him, waiting.

(Why doesn't she try to run away? Is she hypnotized, paralyzed?)

(But where would she run? Now it is too late.)

Stiff-walking Nicola from the barn and into the

farmhouse. No key, he forces the back door by kicking it.

Honeymoon! *Home.*

In the kitchen he instructs Nicola to clean things up. Best as she can. Something must have died here, crawled into the house and died. There is a smell of rot and damp.

Is there a broom?—yes, Nicola discovers a broom.

The Formica-topped kitchen table is still upright, usable, though coated with a film of grime. As he unloads groceries onto it, he hears a soft chattery sound—Nicola's teeth chattering with cold.

Though it is not yet *cold*—not as it will be later, that night.

"Hey! Darling! It's all right. You will be all right. You will see, that is a promise." Very clearly he articulates these words to placate the frightened woman. "We will love each other again."

His expansive voice. His smile. Radiance courses through him. He is excited by the prospect of being *good.*

Too long he has missed being good.

Fuckers have tormented him, keeping him from his good self.

Coaxing a smile from Nicola. Wan, dazed smile. Wants to believe! Her life depends on it.

A banished heir (re)claiming his property, he walks through the farmhouse. Smaller than he recalls. Ceiling lower. Only four—five?—rooms downstairs.

Some of the old furniture is in reasonably good condition, beneath grimy sheets. The walls are badly water-stained, carpets filthy. A closet—moth-eaten blankets, mildewed sheets, towels.

His old room, on the second floor. Filthy floor. Bare mattress, looking as if something has died on it.

Much is familiar to him as a partly recalled dream is familiar. His poor mother! Yet you couldn't love her—you just could not. Hard work, ceaseless work, grim work wore her out. First the spirit, then the body. Insisting on keeping the house clean. Now the house has rebelled against *clean.*

They won't be sleeping in his old room, he has decided. One of the downstairs rooms instead.

Out of the grocery bags they prepare a meal. No electricity in the house of course but canned soup (chicken noodle) is good unheated. Bread, cheese, grape jelly. Peanut butter. Nicola has discovered cups in one of the cupboards and has poured water into two of them.

Despite her nervousness, she is able to eat. Small portions, and her hand trembles. But the husband takes note, this is heartening.

"See? There is hope for us, darling. We can love each other again."

These pronouncements he makes as if someone

were listening. Closely observing and recording.

"We can forgive each other. We can begin again."

Nicola seems in her silence to acquiesce. *Yes.*

She'd always been this sweet, calm girl. Trusting.

That was it—trusting. What he'd loved about her, the trust in her eyes.

The other Nicola, of recent years—she'd dared to doubt him. Turned against him. Denounced him.

But the other, that young Nicola, is her truest self. *She* will return to him now.

As dusk deepens, they huddle together on a sofa in the living room. The (forgiving) husband gathers the (adulterous) wife in his arms.

She doesn't resist. She is meek, obedient. He does not want to think *the shrewd bitch is biding her time until I fall asleep.*

He sings to her, a tuneless tune to comfort. A lullaby. As he'd sung to the infant in its cradle, in his memory.

Though in fact, he'd never glimpsed the infant in its cradle. He'd been thousands of miles away, and he'd never given the infant in its cradle, still less its mother (breasts spilling milk, stretch-marked belly), a second thought.

Nursing mothers, repulsive. *He'd* never had one, he is sure!

But still, an emblem of manhood. His manhood.

"Fathering" a child—virtually every guy in his platoon had.

Casually asks the woman in his arms about her lover. She stiffens. There is no lover.

Of course there is a lover! More than one.

He knows. He has known. Just tell me their names.

In fact, he knows their names. But he wants to hear the names from her.

In a faint voice, she protests, she has no lover. She has never had a lover—except him.

(Is this true? If so, it seems sad to him.)

What about the men she'd betrayed him with?— maybe they don't qualify as *lovers*.

"If they fucked you, that's what counts. *My* wife, another guy fucking."

She shakes her head, no.

She has betrayed him! He laughs. He knows.

She tries to protest, he interrupts her. For many people have reported her behavior to him, while he was in Iraq.

Even a question about whether Meer-me is *his*.

Yes! He's heard that.

She is becoming upset. This is the first he has suggested that his daughter might not be his.

Well, he doesn't believe that rumor. He knows he is the father.

Bond between them. Loves Daddy best.

Eventually the wife will confess about the lovers. Isn't one of them her boss at the college?

He is certain. Running his hands over her cowering body, which is straining away from him now.

The wife is no longer a young wife. Not so beautiful. Or maybe she'd never been beautiful, only just young. Her skin is less soft, the tendons in her neck prominent.

Collarbone, ribs prominent. Has Nicola lost weight to spite *him?*

For sure, her breasts are smaller. Nipples the size of tiny pits retreated into the soft, warm skin, fleeing *him.*

Fact is, today he might not give Nicola a second glance. Sighting her in the 7-Eleven by the high school with her girlfriends. How she'd seen him, too. Dared to smile at him, too.

As if there would be no consequences. From that smile.

Trembling now. Fearful of him now. Respects him now.

But he relents. He will not pursue her just now. Enough for the (guilty) wife to know that the (wronged) husband knows. She will beg forgiveness from him, in time.

Reluctantly she tells him, she must use a bathroom. He helps her to her feet, leads her to the only bathroom in the house, on the first floor. He is obliging, even gentlemanly. This is his house, she is his guest.

The door scarcely shuts. He listens to her inside.

No running water, the (filthy) toilet will not flush. He knows she is embarrassed for she is easily embarrassed. Outside the door he stands guard.

There is a small window in the bathroom, a half window at shoulder height. He is well aware of this window which is why he stands guard at the door.

Of course she will not try to open this window. If this window can be opened. She will not break the window and try to escape.

Ridiculous. Pathetic. He has to smile, the faithless wife is so stymied.

Yet when Nicola steps out of the bathroom and he steps forward to shut the door behind her, something happens: in the periphery of his eye, she disappears.

In an instant, the figure beside him has stepped over the edge of the precipice, vanished.

He shouts, crouches, turns. His eyes narrow to slits. If the razor-honed hunting knife was in his hand, he'd lash out.

Prepared to attack the adversary, approaching him from his blind side.

Except there are two blind sides. He must not allow the wife to step unwittingly into either and disappear from him.

Of course, he locates Nicola immediately. She has never left his side.

Astonished by his sudden alarm, rage. But (wisely) saying nothing.

It is becoming dark. Early October, autumn. Each day shorter than the one before. Each night colder.

On the sofa they have fashioned a kind of nest. Sheets from the closet, a blanket. Even a pillow, to share. Camping out in his own house! In his imaginings on the Greyhound bus, he'd hoped for this, seen it clearly.

But strange, he isn't feeling desire for the woman. Female body so close to his but chilled, stiff. Has it already happened, the female is a corpse?

Gropes for her—breasts, belly. His hand between her thighs.

She shudders, but (wisely) does not wrench away.

But suddenly it happens; he is very tired. Exhausted. The day began a thousand miles away, it seems. Wanted to undress, and undress the woman. But too tired.

His eyelids droop. His limbs go limp, lifeless. He can feel the muscles of his face relax and his mouth ease open. As his breathing deepens, the wife in his arms ceases breathing in sudden stillness, all her senses alert.

Very slowly, cautiously, she detaches herself from him. The heavy arms, legs. She is trembling with excitement, adrenaline like liquid fire coursing through her veins.

But he is too quick for her. Grabs her arm—"Where the fuck are you going?"

He strikes her. Hits her face. Bloodies her nose. Elation in his fists which move of their own volition. At last! At last.

She is sobbing, pleading with him. She wasn't going anywhere, was only trying to be more comfortable . . . He ignores her, yanking at her clothing, tearing what won't give way, baring her belly, thighs, shadowy pubic hair.

"Bitch! Bitch! Liar! Adulteress!"

Unsnaps his khakis, kneeling above her. Gripping her wrists, his muscled legs forcing her legs apart.

It is clumsy, it is not proceeding well. He is red-faced, furious. Feels his face pound with heat. Forcing himself into her—the female. Dry, as dry as parchment paper, dry as sand, she is shut against him, resisting him. She is screaming, sobbing. He will force her, he will enter her. He is grunting, enraged and engorged. *His* wife.

It is quickly ended. Like dry heaving. Gut-wrenching. The woman's will, suffused through her body, which has turned ugly, no softness in it.

"You will burn in Hell."

He clamps his hand over her mouth, her sobbing repulsive to him. He is furious but vindicated, the woman revealing herself to him at last.

Heavily he lies on top of her on the sofa, pinning her down. He will sleep fitfully, in spasms. She will sleep too, or so it seems to him, passing in and out of consciousness, breathing hoarsely through her mouth, for her nose is broken.

At dawn, he is fully awake. In an instant, fully awake. Announces to the sallow, sickly face beneath him that he will be driving her back to Chautauqua Falls.

It has been a failure, their reconciliation. She has not acted in good faith.

She has failed their marriage. She will bear the brunt of the shame.

She is dazed, released from his weight at last. Hardly able to stand. Her hair has become frantic, uncombed.

Rapidly she blinks, trying to see.

He wonders if her eyeballs have hemorrhaged. He'd hit her pretty hard with his fists; both eyes are swollen and blackened.

Exactly how you get arrested. The male. Visible signs of a beating, female face, body. Not good if anyone sees. Reports.

Fortunately, there is *no one*. Not ever again.

He is kind to her, the wounded woman. Walks her to the kitchen, where he soaks a towel with water from one of the plastic bottles, gently pats her swollen face. Why'd she provoke him! Goddamn shame.

He will return her home. Chautauqua Falls. In exchange, he asks her not to contact police. Not to tell anyone.

"Yes!"—almost inaudibly, the woman murmurs.

"Do I have your word? Your vow?"

He does, yes. Almost weeping in gratitude, disbelieving what she has been promised, the woman winces, *yes*.

Crucial to repack the groceries. Even the emptied cans. No trace can be left behind.

Taking away the rumpled, bloodied sheets. Pillow, moth-eaten blanket.

Repacking the car. Dump everything into the trunk. As swift as a knife blade sinking into flesh, the thought comes to him—*Her too. In the trunk. Shut her mouth. Spare yourself.*

But then it seems he has forgotten or decided against this, though driving the car to Round Pond is his new idea, executed with some difficulty as he hasn't remembered exactly where the road is, the narrow gravel road that intersects with Carpenter Road, passes by the pond. But then, by accident (it seems), he locates the pond, sees that indeed it does look deep enough to hide a car, at least at one end—the other is a marsh, cattails.

Also, a lane beside the pond. Farmer's lane, unused for years. But still navigable.

Much effort is required positioning the car on an incline above the pond. Tricky maneuver but can be done. Patience needed. *One breath at a time.*

He'd lain amid carnage not knowing if (in fact) he was still alive. Or what *alive* might even

185

mean. Or whether *alive* was worth it. Long hours, a night and a day, until they'd come to rescue him and some others—broken, mangled bodies, parts of heads. His soul had retreated deep inside his brain like a tiny pit lost in a labyrinth of sponge flesh but it had not (evidently) gone out.

And so, patience now. He has survived until now.

The incline is just steep enough, he can get the car moving. As the woman stands staring in astonishment, he guides the car forward, down, and down, front wheels in the water, then the hood, roof—slow sinking, but sinking.

"Your car is sunk to the depths of Hell. But you have been spared."

The woman is stunned, dull-eyed. Her brain has ceased to function. Bloodied face, bloodied clothing. She looks like the survivor of a car wreck, the husband thinks, tenderly.

He has saved her. She will never know.

"Final Solution"

But now: Final Solution.

All else has failed. Ignominiously.

Out of the backpack—handcuffs.

She backs away, staring. For even with swollen and blackened eyes, she sees.

Purchased in a pawn shop in Stanton, Colorado. Weeks before the Final Solution shaped itself in his brain like a great cumulus cloud.

She tries to resist. Easily he overpowers her. Shuts one of the cuffs around her right wrist and the other around his left wrist.

"See? This is a double lock. So I can trust you."

Linked together now by a small but durable chain of about five inches.

He brandishes the key in his hand. As she stares in disbelief, he tosses it into the pond, where it sinks amid small ripples and is gone.

When she tugs at his arm, panicked, crouching and sobbing, he yanks back, hard.

"No. That's ended—who you thought you were. We're together now."

Grimly he lifts his arm to discipline her. To allow her to know that if he wishes, he can dislocate her arm at the shoulder with a sudden, violent yank.

She whimpers in pain, helpless. He lowers his arm, the pain is lessened.

Such power over the woman! Too long he'd deprived himself of the pleasure of authority.

But there is no need to terrify her, he thinks. Now that the end is approaching.

She stammers, trying to speak. *Why . . . why . . . What are . . .* But her throat is raw and hoarse, her words unintelligible.

She is oddly crouched, her knees bent. The handcuffs have brought them close together now, as husband and wife should be. Merest tug of the husband's arm, the wife is thrown off balance, toward him.

"You are my wife. That will never change. Anything that was going to happen, to change us, is ended now."

Like a doomed creature resisting the collar around its neck, she stiffens instinctively.

But really, there is no resisting. No choice about yielding to him. Unless she stumbles, falls, and then he might drag her. The pain in her wrist and arm will be excruciating.

The husband seems to have a plan. Leading her around the pond, passing the marshy area where black-feathered birds scream at them indignantly.

It is a measure of great dismay to her that the roof of her car isn't visible through the water, at least from shore. That the vehicle has sunk so swiftly, leaving no trace.

Her car. The first she'd owned by herself, in her lifetime.

But where is Lew leading her? Vaguely it seems that they are headed back toward the farmhouse on Carpenter Road.

Unless she is confused. Unless she has been turned around.

Oh but he must have a second key to the handcuffs!—she tells herself.

He is *not a bad person*—she tells herself.

Trying to believe that in some way he is leading her back home. The house on Grant Street, Chautauqua Falls, where their daughter is (anxiously) waiting for her. Where Dominique waits with Miriam, waiting for Mommy to return. Hadn't he promised her . . .

A protective haze has begun to drift over her brain.

Desperate to believe. To her shame, her heart leaped in hope, in the wild elation of hope.

As she tries to match her steps to his. The man's long legs. Even with his limp, his wounded leg, the man can move with surprising swiftness.

It is cruel of him, calculating, that he moves just fast enough to keep her off balance, staggering. And so close to him! From a little distance it might appear that they are holding hands.

Long ago, walking with Lew, his big hand enclosing hers. Pulling her along, tugging.

Why?—no reason. Or maybe he didn't notice.

He liked her to show affection for him in public. And his hand on her bare arm, her knee. Thigh. *His.*

Taunting her now. Tormenting her. Laughs at her, the misery in her face.

"Now I can trust you. Now, if I fall asleep, you ain't gonna run away."

Ain't gonna is uttered in his mock-Southern accent. Something he'd picked up in Iraq.

He has left behind the white painter's cap. The paint-splotched denim jacket. Wearing now just a soiled T-shirt, paint-splotched khakis, hiking boots. Between his shoulder blades the back-pack is askew. One of the water bottles that he has forced partway into a zippered compartment threatens to fall out.

But none of the groceries. Left in the trunk of her car, sunk beneath the insect-stippled surface of Round Pond.

"Why—why are you"—Nicola can barely speak, her throat is aflame—*"doing this to me . . ."*

He doesn't answer at first. He is pleased with himself, satisfied. A smile twitches about his mouth inside the tattered whiskers.

At last he says, in the tone of one passing judgment: "It isn't about you, Nicola. It's about *us.*"

Adding, in his taunting way, "*She* told me. How you'd betrayed me."

The wife shakes her head *no.* That cannot be true.

Does he mean Miriam? Meer-me? The child? Not possible.

"See, I asked her if Mommy had a special friend who came to visit her when I was gone, a man friend, and she said *yes*. Mommy did."

Nicola is horrified. Nicola protests. *"No no no. Not possible . . ."*

Can't breathe through her nose. Gasping for breath. Her brain begins to swoon. Yet she means to be stoic. She will not give in.

Will not beg the gloating man—*No! I never betrayed you! Let me go.*

Pulling her forward. Though he is panting too, sweating through his clothes.

For hours they make their way through the Shaheen countryside. Pastures that have reverted to wilderness, deciduous forests where half the trees are broken, storm-damaged. Brambles, thorns catch at their clothes and skin.

At last, following a faint path along a narrow creek, fast-running in the aftermath of recent rainstorms.

"D'you know where we are? This is my property."

He must mean it is part of the farmland owned by his family, or once owned by them. In his face, above the matted and snarled beard, a look of mounting excitement, certitude.

Abruptly he stops, as if he has just thought of something. Orders Nicola to help him swing the backpack from his shoulders, letting it fall to the ground.

In an awkward maneuver, using just his right, free hand, he manages to unzip one of the compartments. Nicola sees in astonishment that Lew is removing a gun from the backpack—a revolver with a carved wooden handle.

Must be the gun he'd claimed to have won in a poker game. She'd never been allowed to see it clearly, only glimpsed it. She'd insisted that Lew could not keep it in the house unless it was unloaded and locked securely away.

He'd complied, or so she'd thought. Wherever the gun was hidden, she hadn't known. Though he'd laughed when she told him the gun must be unloaded—*What the fuck's the point of an unloaded gun?*

Nicola's heart is pounding violently. Pulses in her head like drumbeats. What had she been thinking, to have lived with this man for as long as she had? Why such a mistake? Of course, one day he would use that gun on her.

Yet Lew surprises her again: unpredictably rears back, swings his arm with a grunt, tosses the gun into the creek.

Laughing at Nicola, her confusion. She cannot comprehend—what is he doing?

He takes up the backpack, carrying it in his hand. The bottle of water has fallen out, forgotten. He tugs her forward. Pleased with himself, talking to himself. Urgency in his behavior.

"When they find us, they will understand. This is the only way."

The immediate fear she'd felt at the sight of the gun is slow to abate. Her legs have begun to ache. Her feet. Her shoes are thin-soled, nothing like Lew's sturdy hiking boots. She can't go much farther, she will soon sink to her knees. He will have to drag her.

Lew appears to be following the meandering creek. Amid her misery, Nicola feels a faint throb of hope—*He is leading us back to the house . . .*

No. He is seeking a place, she can see how his eyes dart about.

Beside the creek, a clearing. Ahead is a dense pinewoods. Once, there was a path here, a fishermen's path perhaps. The place is shot with a luminous autumnal light. Curious scattering of unusually large rocks, as if purposefully arranged as in a totemic ritual.

She sees in his face, he has found it now. Here.

Lew stops. Squats. His face too is luminous. Creased in concentration. He is scarcely aware of her now, as she is forced to kneel beside him. With his right hand he manages to remove, from the backpack, a hunting knife.

This too she recognizes. In horror her dimmed eyes seize upon it.

Eight-inch, stainless steel, Japanese-made—the hunting knife he'd sometimes kept in the glove compartment of their car along with a flashlight, a driver's manual.

"When they find you, they will see you were spared."

Reproachful emphasis on *you*.

Frowning, his face oozing sweat, Lew brings the tip of the knife blade against the inside of his left arm. Mere inches from Nicola, who strains away from him trembling.

Cannot turn away her eyes. Staring, blinking— the sight of the blade has mesmerized her . . .

Slowly, deliberately, he draws the blade along the length of a thick-pulsing blue artery. When bright blood begins to appear, swiftly running down his arm, dripping into the grass, he cries aloud joyously as Nicola screams, jerking as far from him as she can, trying frantically to escape.

Lew laughs, there is no pain! No pain! He insists.

Continuing with the precision of a surgeon, drawing the blade along the bloodied arm, which quivers, quakes, even as it is held firm against his left knee.

Impervious to pain. Pain is *his*.

He is grim, gloating. He is bereft of fear. Fear of death, of the unknown—he has transcended these.

Bleeding from several wounds in his left arm, suffused with energy, Lew swings his right arm, throws the bloodied hunting knife into the creek.

Nicola is sobbing, hysterical. She has pulled away from the bleeding man as much as she can, her arm outstretched, her wrist wracked in pain.

She is not fully conscious, the horror is so great. Spurting blood, the man's blood, slippery on her, so distraught she comes to think that he has slashed her too, that she too is bleeding, helpless now as the grasses, the ground soak up the blood.

Is the man laughing, or is this a keening sound, an ululation like the death cry of a wild creature, terrible to hear?

Mad. He is mad.

So close to madness, she will be infected with it.

Madness of his blood, on her.

Nicola has fainted, her head rolling against soft, wet earth.

Never again will she regain consciousness as herself.

How many minutes, hours. As he yields to *it*.

Frantic to escape it. But she cannot.

Calling for help, screaming. Fits of hysteria, rage. Her throat is scraped raw. Her vision has become a narrow tunnel, edged with shadow.

Will she die—like this?

In this place? Shackled to the husband's corpse?

With part of her mind she is still able to think

clearly. A small candle flame, tremulous. She understands the husband's motives. Why he has done what he has done. His purpose. His curse.

Exsanguination. The wonder of it. Inexorable, unstoppable.

Pool of dark blood cooling around the body. Nicola cannot escape.

How still Lew has become! The mad gloating soon fades, the murmurings dim to silence.

Labored breathing, fainter and fainter. To silence.

And Nicola, exhausted and obliterated. Shackled to the body as it cools.

Desperate to yank her badly bruised wrist out of the metal cuff, she turns her wrist, turning and twisting, sobbing, hysterical, doomed.

Her skin is abraded, bleeding. Possibly the wrist is sprained. Like a frantic animal, she would gnaw off her hand to escape.

Once, as a child, hearing of how a young fox escaped a steel trap by gnawing off its foreleg. Can't remember—she might have actually seen the pitiful severed leg . . .

Her teeth in her own flesh would be weak, ineffectual. Hopeless.

So close to the lifeless man's arm, she cannot bear it.

Even with weight loss, Lew must weigh more than two hundred pounds. Twice Nicola's weight. Tremendous effort is required to pull the body in this place even a few inches through the dense grass.

Passing in and out of consciousness. Dazed, her face swollen. Insects have been sucking her blood—mosquitoes, gnats. She is faint with hunger, her throat parched with thirst even as she is losing such words as *hunger, thirst.*

Her immediate effort is dragging the body to the creek. Left arm stretched out, the weight of the body pulling against her wrist, threatening to pull her arm out of its socket. So tired! Not twenty-four hours have passed; this has been eternity.

The better part of an hour is required to drag the body close enough to the creek that she might lower her head to the rushing water, attempt to drink.

Like a frantic animal flicking her tongue against the water. Nothing else matters except assuaging the terrible thirst.

Weight of the corpse. Deadweight.

Limbs sprawled, mouth open. The most bitter joke, the man has been transformed into a body, an object. Obscene in death, hateful.

The husband's revenge. She understands.

Ghastly face that she'd once considered handsome. Grayish skin, tattered and discolored whiskers. Unfocused eyes, covered in a kind of film, that seem yet to be observing her. And the slack mouth, jeering.

She is sick with horror. The body will decay.

She will be the witness. Never can she escape.

No idea where they are. In which direction there is a road—any road. And how far from any human habitation—no idea.

Along Carpenter Road, abandoned and shuttered houses. Decaying barns. Little traffic.

Yet in her weak, faltering voice she calls for help. Even as she understands the effort is hopeless.

Seeing now, he'd thrown away the gun so that she could not use it on herself. He'd thrown away the knife so that she could not use it on herself.

Rigor mortis. The stiffening of the body. She has turned her face away from the loathsome thing; never will she allow herself to look at it again.

Blood staining her clothing. Blood on her arms, her face. Blood drying in her hair. Nightmare buzzing of flies.

Help! Help me! Help . . .

From a little distance she hears herself. How weak, piteous.

No help—the man is laughing at her.

(Is Lew alive? Has he been pretending to be dead?)

(So recently having died, is it possible to return to the living—to life? In her delirium Nicola seems to recall that this might be so.)

With each minute the body is beginning to break down. What is physical must decay. Bacteria, a buzz of flies, inexorable decomposition.

Already the smell of it has begun to sicken her. Rancid, rotting meat. She will not be able to bear the horror that is imminent.

Must maneuver herself, her face, as far from the body as she can. If there is a wind, she must be upwind from it.

If only she could drag the body into the creek, to cause it to sink beneath the surface of the water, she might escape the stench . . . but she cannot, she will be drawn into the water herself, to drown.

Not even that solace will be possible for her, Nicola thinks.

Revenge. But by now she has lost the word.

Wait, wait! Black-feathered birds are mocking her in the foliage overhead.

Coming to peck out the dead man's eyes. And then her eyes.

In terror of vultures. If they mistake her for a corpse while she is still alive . . .

Frightened by the black-feathered birds, she is empowered with sudden strength. Wrenching her arm another time, twisting her wrist so cleverly, turning the (now thin, bony) wrist in such a way that she can slip free just as the first of the birds swoops down to peck at her face . . .

Screams at them. Birds of hell. *Go away, go away! I am still alive.*

• • •

But no. Wait. It occurs to Nicola one midday, one hour, that the rotting is a good thing. A blessing.

How had she failed to understand? How—so *stupid?*

The arm to which she is shackled, the hand, the wrist will rot. As soon as the flesh begins to turn soft, she will be able to tug the handcuff away from it.

Excited, hopeful. Where there has been no hope, now there comes a sudden bright, ecstatic hope, as sparkling as a fountain.

Eventually the hateful body so close beside hers will become a skeleton. The flesh will rot, melt away. This is a promise. It will not be difficult at all to extricate herself from mere bones . . .

(Are they in bed together? In their old bed, on Grant Street? Sometimes it seems to Nicola yes, no time has passed at all. *Husband and wife* still.)

But no. Nicola will not be alive when the body becomes a skeleton. Or, if Nicola is living, it will be a bare, minimal life of flickering consciousness.

No strength, no will. No Nicola.

In a swoon of despair. Sinking.

She is becoming weaker, more defeated. As days pass and nothing changes even as everything has changed and will continue to change, she is held captive.

In the befouled, bloodied grasses, lying

stretched out motionless as the loathsome corpse itself. As far from the decaying body as possible. Turning her face away, trying to breathe. She is feverish, her heart beats erratically. Pain from the raw, wounded wrist shoots toward her heart.

She will die of raging infection, she thinks. Her arm swollen, wrist swollen so that the cruel metal will cut into it.

Is that a more painful death than death by (slow, inexorable) starvation?

Fever, delirium. Hallucinations.

She has fouled her clothing, urine, excrement. No escaping the horrors of the body.

But here is a reprise of some sort—as in a blurred film she is able to see her first meeting with the man.

When she was seventeen—so young! And Lew, a few years older.

In the 7-Eleven store near the high school. Long-limbed, insolent Lew Hayman staring at Nicola, though it was one of her friends who'd called out to him—*Hey Lew! Hi.*

That rush of excitement, almost faintness, seeing Lew Hayman's eyes on her. Smile aimed at her.

This time she shrinks from that smile. Hurries away, leaves the store. Stammers an excuse, she has to go home.

He calls after her, she doesn't hear.

Run! Run from him.

In this way, her life is saved.

• • •

. . . waking from the heavy stupor of fever-sleep to hear voices.

She sits up. She is eager, excited. Her voice that has been unused for days is returned to her.

Help me! Over here! I am here! Help . . .

At a little distance in the pinewoods, two figures. Hunters? In Day-Glo orange vests? A father and a son?

Hesitantly the two approach as she continues to call to them—*Help! Help me* . . . She cringes seeing their uplifted rifles.

Waving to them with her free hand. On her knees, trying to stand but pulled down by the weight of the body.

Hello! Here! I am here . . .

Cautiously they approach. (And is there a third hunter, also in a bright orange vest?)

She is uneasy. The hunters carry their rifles uplifted.

In their faces she sees horror. She sees dismay, disgust.

It is the body sprawled in the grasses they see, in its state of decomposition. Beetles, flies, maggots. Slick, shiny, putrescent, stinking flesh out of which blackened eye sockets stare.

Jesus! What is it?—a dead man?

. . . dead man, and a woman . . .

Standing over Nicola. But why are they staring at the body without seeming to see her?

Why don't they hear her as she begs them?

Standing over her. A man, a younger man. Father, son. Why do their eyes glide over her without seeming to see her?

Why do they not hear Nicola as she begs them? *Help me! Take me with you! Cut away his hand! I am still alive . . .*

Her throat is so raw from screaming, blood gushes into her mouth.

Hot skin, fevered skin. Deafening buzzing of insects. She is very ill, confused. Her head pounds. Her brain has become porous, infected by airborne bacteria, spores of rot.

Shakes her head to clear it and wake herself, but there is no one there.

The hunters? Where have they gone?

The father and son in Day-Glo hunting vests? The shadowy third, approaching? She'd seen them so clearly—vividly . . .

Sobbing in disappointment, despair. She'd come so close to being saved.

But then, another time: summoning what remains of her strength to reach around into one of the khaki pockets of the rotting corpse behind her, at which she cannot look, groping blindly, thrilled when her fingers discover a small key.

The second key to the handcuffs!

She'd known there had to be a second key. Lew would not have thrown away both keys.

He'd intended for her to find it. So like the husband, to play one of his mean tricks.

Not easy, it requires dexterity and courage, inserting the key in the lock, which is coated with blood. Like threading a needle with a very small eye. Showing Miriam how threading a needle is accomplished, but her hand is shaking . . .

But here is the mistake. The lock is coated with (dried, calcified) blood.

She must lick the lock clean. Lick away the blood with her tongue.

Ugly taste, yes, but she has no choice. Freedom is so close she can almost smell it.

Yet—the dried blood is slow to vanish. Rust-tasting, salty. Her mouth is so dry.

Yet—in triumph after some minutes, the blood has been licked away—Nicola is able to use the key to unlock the cuffs.

The manacles fall away into the grass.

And the rotting body falls heavily away.

Nicola is free!—hardly able to stand, for her knees are racked with pain. But she is upright, she has saved herself.

Faint with hunger, making her way along the creek. Stooping to sink her face into the cool, rushing water, drinking like a thirsty dog.

Her fingers pluck at berries, shoving them into her mouth. Hardly more than wizened pits.

After how many days, at last pushing her way through the underbrush. Thorns tear at her exposed arms, her face. The sheerest luck, Nicola emerges at the side of a road.

The (unpaved) Carpenter Road!

Soon, then, headlights.

For it is dusk. The day has slipped beneath the horizon.

In the road, waving, screaming. Soundless screams.

The vehicle stops abruptly. *Jesus! What's this . . .*

Taking pity on her in her dazed, emaciated state. Eyes swollen near shut with insect bites. Clothes torn, blood-splattered. So weak. They try to give her water, and she drinks thirstily, then begins to vomit.

Nothing to vomit, dry heaving.

Are you alone, ma'am? Is somebody with you?

Better get you to a hospital . . .

Can you tell us who you are? Do you have a name?

Rough ride on the unpaved road. Twisting, curving road in the foothills of the Chautauqua mountains. Her spirit detaches itself from the lurching and jarring of the van. Hovers above her broken body in the back seat of the vehicle. Unrecognizable face, bloodless lips. Barely alive and yet—alive.

She begs them, take me home. Not the hospital but home.

My little girl, my daughter!—take me to her, I love her so much.

They are reluctant. They quarrel with each other. Yet soon afterward there is Miriam, before her. So that Nicola knew, Miriam was close by all along.

Frightened yet hopeful that Mommy has come home.

Mommy has been missing so long, but Meer-me never gave up hope. Hugging Mommy, and Mommy hugs her. Not even the need for tears. Mommy is beyond tears.

She will be trading her life for Miriam's life. Of course, this is what a mother would do. This is what a mother does. It is obvious, unquestioned, what a mother does.

Removing the little silver ring with the cloudy pale-blue opal from her finger where it has been dangerously loose. The ring her grandmother entrusted to her. Slipping it on the child's largest finger, middle finger of her right hand.

Of course, the ring is too large for a five-year-old's finger. Mommy will wind a sliver of transparent tape through it, to adjust it.

Oh honey—I didn't leave you. I never left you, I was here with you all the time.

IV

Testimony

Looked like just bones at first. I mean—animal bones.

You see this sometimes in the country. In a field. Where an animal has died, laid down and died, or another animal killed it and ate its flesh and there's just—remains . . .

But these were different. You could see.

Two skeletons—two skulls. Not far apart.

One skull was bigger than the other, this was the Daddy-skull. The smaller skull was the Mommy-skull.

But—is this true? For at first she couldn't tell. At first her astonished eyes saw just bones—dull white, discolored, scattered in the tall, gone-to-seed grasses.

And this too is not true. For at first you don't see bones. *You are eight years old. You have no idea what you are seeing.*

Only later will the terrible words come to you.

Bones, skulls. Human skeletons.

Handcuffs.

The Convalescent

She is telling Willem all that she has never told anyone.

All that she has dreamed, imagined. Held captive, as if her (right) wrist is manacled to another whose face she cannot see.

In stunned silence, Willem listens. Whatever he might have imagined Abby to be keeping to herself, he could never have imagined what he has been hearing.

As poisonous liquid has dripped from his young wife's supine body in the bed in intensive care, drained by a catheter into a plastic container beneath the bed, so now poison drains from her soul as he grips her hand.

Soon! It will be over soon.

Abby, don't give up.

She shuts her eyes, exhausted. Hours each day in rehab, her body relearning the instinctive skills it has lost.

Lifting, straightening, flexing her legs. Exercises with weights. Exercises with dumbbells. Relearning how to breathe properly.

Often she is in despair. She will never walk normally again. For what is walking but having faith that, propelled forward, we will not teeter and fall; we will not lose our balance, lurch and sway like a drunkard. The very mystery of *balance*.

Tears streak Abby's cheeks. She weeps without restraint. Willem withdraws from her, knowing she needs to be alone.

So long she'd refused to recall her lost childhood. Her lost mother, who'd died so horribly.

Five weeks since the accident. Or has it been six?

Discharged from the hospital, now in the adjoining rehab clinic.

One day at a time! One breath at a time, Abby recalls.

Headaches feel as if her skull is split in two. The punctured lung heals slowly. She is susceptible to lung infections, her white blood count dangerously low.

Willem has donated blood for Abby: they have the identical blood type, O.

(A sign from God? Willem wants to think so.)

(Though lately Willem isn't so sure about God. He believes in Jesus, who remains his closest friend, but not so much in God, who is as capricious and unjust as a human father and cannot be trusted.)

Praying for his young wife, suffused with the ferocity of love.

In warm May sunshine Willem pushes Abby in the wheelchair. Stopping so that she can lift herself from the chair with her arms, balance herself on her feet, try to *walk*.

Oh, Abby is breathless, as excited as a young child! Her husband watches her with love, the most ardent and selfless love, as a father might watch his own child learning to walk for the first time.

Take my hand, Abby!—Willem urges.

But Abby wants to manage on her own, as far as she can. Biting her lower lip in concentration, determined not to stagger, fall.

A relapse. E. coli infection, punctured (left) lung.

Swarming bacteria, malevolent and rapacious.

For five days Abby drifts in a fever fugue, rehospitalized. Her skin becomes sallow again; she loses the meager weight she has regained. IV fluids in her bruised arms. Another time, the machine pumping cool oxygen into her lungs, a monitor close beside the bed. Another time the catheter inserted into her bladder, the plastic bag beneath the bed filling with toxic liquid waste.

Did you think we would forget you? We would never forget you.

Still, we are waiting for you. We will never not be waiting for you.

Bouts of sadness, sorrow. Post-trauma, her body hurtled into the street like a rag doll, what can she expect?

A voice chides her: "You came close to dying,

Abby. You must know that. Recovery will take time. We are doing all that we can, but you must help, too."

(Who is telling her this? Her eyes are shut tight, her jaws clenched, holding onto her life with all her strength.)

You must give up your delusions, Abby. This "husband" of yours!—there is no husband.

(Eyes shut. Breath inheld. Fists gripping the sweaty sheets. *No.*)

What a joke, Abby! Abby isn't even your name. Gabriella—look who's putting on airs! You are Miriam, plain little orphan Miriam. No one would ever marry you, *Abby. No one would ever love* you. *A daughter who betrayed her own mother, a daughter who'd been Daddy's girl, what a joke that anyone could love* you.

Waking to the misery of fever, confusion. Her mouth so dry she can't swallow without whimpering in pain. Her heart is hammering, and one of the night nurses gives her an injection to sedate her.

Willem isn't here—she blinks, tries to see.

Was there ever a Willem?—a *husband?*

It was said in Chautauqua Falls that Miriam's parents had abandoned her, but not at the same time.

Often Miriam was asked what else her mother had said to her before disappearing from

Chautauqua Falls, but Miriam was just a little girl, five years old at the time, and she cried easily.

Miriam learned that if you cry, questions will cease. If you cry quickly, questions will cease quickly.

How many times, numbly shaking her head *No, no*—she doesn't remember.

She'd told them the crucial lie, however: her mother promised her she would be back.

Wandering the countryside. The old farm at Shaheen. Along the shallow creek, a faint path.

A mile along the creek, the skeletons await her. She will understand only much later how the skeletons called to her.

Meer-me! Meer-me!

Still, she can hear them. In the hospital bed, in the numbed days, weeks to follow. Keeping the beat of her heart.

She was forbidden to explore the hay barn with the rotting roof, the collapsed silo that was a hive of scuttling rats, and the "pond" by the cow barn that stank of manure years after the herd was sold, and she had no wish to explore the ruins of the chicken coop that in damp weather exuded an odor so vile it was nearly visible, a shuddering in the air.

Discovering the bones. Ghost white in the tall grasses buzzing with insects. You see, but you don't see.

Look again, but no, look away.

Don't see, but you see.

Come closer.

What am I seeing?—I am seeing my aunt Traci's face.

*It is a creased face, like something left out in the rain. But it is a kind face, a face that smiles, eyes that smile so you want to scream at her—*Stop!

I was not truthful to you, Willem. Before we were married.

I did not tell the truth about my aunt Traci, no more than I did about my mother and my father.

Because I loved you, and I did not want to lose your love.

My aunt Traci sacrificed so much for me. I was never grateful.

When my mother abandoned me, my aunt Traci took me in without question. Soon, then, her life began to fall apart.

She began drinking. She lost her teaching job. She was evicted from her house. A man she'd loved took advantage of her, took money from her and vanished. I had to think it was because of me, and also because of my father, who was my aunt's brother.

What he'd done, the shame of it. The shock. What they'd been led to think he'd done. Not knowing that he had not killed himself in Wyoming, but would kill himself months later, on his family's property in Shaheen.

Himself, and my mother. And no one would know except me.

From time to time that summer, her aunt Traci roused herself to bathe, brush her unruly graying hair, apply lipstick with shaky fingers. "Dress"—in the least badly stained shirt, slacks. Open-toed sandals betraying ugly female feet. Ask Miriam if her breath smelled, and Miriam shook her head *no*.

From an early age, eager to utter those words adults crave to hear.

How you come to be *loved*. Avoid being *abandoned*.

Drive to Shaheen Falls, to the drugstore, grocery store. Tremulous hands, nerves twitching in her face, needs a drink or drinks, an hour, two hours, three hours at the Red Bull Inn on the highway, where she was observed sitting alone in a booth, not young, though also not bad-looking, a sort of dour schoolteacher face, flat chest, thick hips, lipstick-red mouth, nursing a succession of ales while outside, in her rust-stippled old Ford, the lonely child rumored to be her niece, rumored to be the orphan daughter of that bastard Llewyn Hayman who'd blown his brains out somewhere in Wyoming, waited with the patience of the doomed, reading, or pretending to read, a water-logged children's book.

Approached by a stranger, strangers, asked if

she'd like company, answer always blunt, sar-castic monosyllables. *No. Thank. You.*

Fifteen years later in her hospital bed recalling her aunt calling to her, fretful and forlorn—*Miriam! Miriam . . .*

In the doorway of the old farmhouse, cigarette in hand. A woman's ruined life. Who's to blame? No one.

Miriam, where are you? Please, sweetie—your auntie Traci loves you.

Crawling so the squinting aunt couldn't see. Hiding behind the silo that exuded a powerful fermented smell. Tossing rocks into the putrid barnyard pond to frighten away horseflies.

Only waiting for the bones to call to her. Thrilled, scarcely able to breathe, waiting.

Snarled hair, stained clothes. Like inflamed freckles on her face and arms, reddened bites of mosquitoes, ticks.

Of course she would make her way along the lane. Between the overgrown fields, a mile to the shallow creek.

Bones in the tall grasses, unmistakably. How many times discovered.

Shreds of rotted clothing, a shoe nearly buried in mud. So many years later, she has lost count.

Why had she never told her aunt Traci what she discovered? Why has she never told anyone?

Compelled to return to the skeletons, to refute

what she'd seen. For each time—running back to the house, to her aunt Traci, who'd by then given up calling for her and had gone inside to drink in the dark—she would come to doubt her senses.

She knew, yet she did not know.

She didn't know, had no way of really knowing. Yet she knew.

The bald Daddy-skull, grimacing in anger.

The Mommy-skull, smaller. So very quiet, near-hidden in the grass, waiting.

Shaheen

"Today. We'll drive there."

Abby has been discharged from the rehab clinic. From now on she will have therapy as an outpatient.

Good news! Abby weeps in Willem's arms.

"Should we? Are you ready?"

Is she ready? *No.*

"Yes."

For weeks Willem has been vowing, one day they will drive to Shaheen. To her grandparents' old farm. He will hike along the creek, search for the skeletons beside the creek.

He will go alone. He is determined. If there is anything to be found after fifteen years, Willem will find it.

Abby knows she must defer to fate. She does not believe in God, nor even in Jesus, but she believes in fate. She will defer to her husband's wishes. She understands that the skeletons must be discovered—and identified. If they exist.

A phase of her life is ending. She has been discharged from the clinic. She is no longer a patient, an invalid. Her body's white blood cells have overcome the invading bacteria.

Risking so much. Baring her heart to the stranger who is her husband.

"Yes. I'm ready."

And so, in a vehicle borrowed from one of Willem's brothers they drive two hundred miles south and west from Hammond, into the foothills of the Chautauqua mountains. They drive through the town of Chautauqua Falls without stopping, directly south to Shaheen on the old state highway.

As Willem drives, he holds Abby's hand in his right hand, his young wife's chilled fingers clutching at his own.

Abby provides directions. After so many years, her memory of the Shaheen countryside is returning.

A hilly landscape crisscrossed with ditches, streams. Those hills—called "drumlins"—formed long ago by glaciers. Through the foliage Abby has a glimpse of a large pond set back from the road—Round Pond, her aunt Traci called it.

Stay away from Round Pond!—her aunt warned her.

But why?

There're *water snakes* there—that's why.

Abby shudders, recalling. She'd never gone anywhere near Round Pond.

They are approaching the old farm, Abby senses. Her heart has begun to beat rapidly, she is suffused with a sensation of excitement and dread.

Water snakes. She has not thought of *water snakes* since leaving Chautauqua Falls.

Guiltily she wonders what has become of her aunt Traci. Abby has only heard second and third hand, from her cousin Noreen, whose accounts of relatives can hardly be trusted.

The property on Carpenter Road was eventually foreclosed by a bank in Chautauqua Falls. The mortgage had gone unpaid for months. Debts. Everything lost, abandoned. Medical bills, car payments, poor Traci barely managed to keep up.

For years she'd lived in Chautauqua Falls, sharing a duplex with another woman, each of them employed by the school district as substitute teachers. In time Traci would move away, to Port Oriskany on the southern shore of Lake Ontario, where no one knew the name Hayman. Her heart had been broken. Her beloved niece Miriam had left Chautauqua Falls as soon as she graduated from high school and never again called Traci and never wrote.

She will make up for it now, Abby thinks. She is so ashamed!

Sick with guilt, she'd never told her aunt Traci that she was engaged. Never so much as considered inviting Traci to the wedding. Had she even informed Traci that she'd gone to live in Hammond?

In her senior year in high school, a revulsion for her old life had swept over her, she could not endure continuing as Miriam Hayman, the girl whose father had killed himself somewhere out west and whose mother had gone to find him— driving in her own car, alone and without a word of explanation or goodbye.

And both of them missing, gone. Just—*gone.*

She could not bear it, being pitied. She could not bear *Miriam.*

On sheets of paper she wrote her new, beautiful name—the name of no one in her life and no one of whom she'd ever heard—*Gabriella.*

No one from Chautauqua Falls knew Gabriella, or Abby. Her new life was her secret.

Guiding Willem along Carpenter Road, which is still unpaved, badly rutted.

Fifteen years! Yet little seems to have changed. The mountainous counties of southwestern New York State have been economically distressed for decades, much farmland abandoned.

Though there is at least one dairy farm remaining on Carpenter Road. Abby sees a small herd of Holsteins in a pasture, grazing. Nearest neighbors of the Haymans half a mile away.

There!—Abby catches sight of the farmhouse, which is badly rotted, partially collapsed. Larger than she recalls, for she'd rarely seen the house from the road at such a distance; she would not have remembered that there was a front veranda with beveled posts and missing floorboards, sunken now into tall grasses and underbrush. She would not have remembered an ancient lightning rod on the highest peak of the roof, askew but still standing.

The property now belongs to a Chautauqua Falls bank. In the front yard is an upright FOR SALE sign partly hidden by weeds.

Abby feels a stab of longing, sorrow—for her aunt Traci, who'd brought her here impulsively, irresponsibly, it was charged. *That drunk woman, what is she thinking! That poor child.*

Well, no one could camp out in this house now. Not even Miriam's aunt Traci.

Willem parks the car, not in the overgrown driveway, but on the road in front of the house. He is excited, elated.

"So you lived here! My farm girl."

Abby laughs, startled. She'd thought she had explained that she'd stayed in this house for only a single, desperate summer.

More solemnly Willem says: "We have to do this now, Abby. You have to be free of this."

Willem, who prepares conscientiously for everything, has prepared for his hike into the Shaheen countryside. He is wearing a long-sleeved shirt and long pants tucked into hiking boots to discourage ticks. He has bottled water, a camera, and his cell phone. He has even trimmed back his beard, oddly curly now, giving his lower face a look of determination. The boy she'd first glimpsed in the County Services building,

scarcely a year earlier, rawboned, adolescent—
that boy seems to have vanished.

Willem will take photographs of whatever it is
he finds. If there is evidence of a crime, he will
bring these photographs to the state police. It is
something that must be done, he believes.

Willem's morality is clear-cut. There are things
that *must be done*. And so, there are those who
must do them.

Abby volunteers to draw a map for Willem. It
is all there, in her head—the memory of the lanes
bordering the pastures, the sagging barbed wire
fences, the creek that had no name. (Did the creek
have a name? No one had ever told her.) She can
recall a ravine filled with rocks somewhere on
the property, which she'd tried to explore just
once and cut one of her knees badly.

The map is simple, as a child might draw it.
Exactly where the path is, or had once been.
Approximately how far before Willem will see
the creek. And how far beyond that, turning to
the left, he will see something white glimmering
in the grasses that he won't be able to identify at
first, until he comes closer.

If he follows the creek, he will find the scattered bones. If they exist.

Almost giddy with excitement, Willem kisses
Abby. She isn't sure that she likes this. Almost,
she wishes she had never told her husband what
has festered in her heart.

A risk, to open your heart to a stranger.

"So, Abby—wait here. I'll be back."

Never a thought that Abby might accompany him. She isn't strong enough yet for such a hike. Her legs would collapse beneath her after a mile.

No, no! She cannot.

Her knees have grown weak. She finds a place to sit. In the ruins of the house, at the rear.

Remains of a small porch on which there was a rain barrel. Beside a lilac tree with curiously twisted limbs.

Yes, she remembers. The sweet smell of lilac, which brings a rush of tears to her eyes.

Wipes at her eyes. But she will not weaken.

Watches her husband stride along the lane. Long legs, straw-colored hair, broad shoulders.

Willem stops, turns. Waves at her. How brave her young husband seems, embarked upon an adventure! Abby waves to him; she hears the sound of frightened laughter issuing from her own mouth.

Love love love love you.

She recalls her father, tapping at the window of her room. Kissing the windowpane and smearing it with his mouth—funny Daddy! He'd made her laugh, and he'd made her cry.

The barrette he'd given her. Or rather, Dominique had given her, from Daddy. *He says happy birthday.*

Just a pink plastic barrette, from a drugstore. A

barrette she'd lost, but later she'd bought another, identical one for herself. And that barrette she'd lost, too.

Her mother's ring. The cloudy-blue opal. Mommy had promised, this ring is for you when your finger is big enough.

She wears only one ring, the Celtic wedding band on her left hand. That is enough for her, Abby thinks.

Alone at the rear of the ruined house, Abby thinks of such matters. Observing the slow, calm progress of her thoughts—like high-scudding cumulus clouds, filmy white, not sick-bloated thunderheads darkening the sky.

She has been discharged from the clinic now, just three days. Three nights she has been sleeping with her husband in their bed.

Her heart quickens at the realization—*their bed*.

In waves, the knowledge washes over her; she is no longer a virgin, but a married woman. Like the vision of skeletons that look as if they are dancing in the grasses, this realization is almost too immense to be absorbed.

In their bed in Willem's arms she has had difficulty sleeping. She is certain that she will never sleep so close to another person, feeling that person's breath on her face. And Willem twitches and sighs and snores and kicks. And the hairs on his chest are wiry, ticklish. And his whiskers—scratchy against her sensitive skin. Yet Abby has slept three nights in succession. Not through the night, but intermittently, in abrupt fugues of sleep, more than she expected.

Willem kisses her avidly, hungrily. She is astonished by his love for her and by his desire for her, which she observes as one might observe a raging fire from just a few feet away, dangerously close.

She loves him, though she is just slightly frightened of him.

Is he hurting her? Willem asks worriedly.

No. He is not hurting her, she assures him.

He's afraid of hurting her, Willem says. He is afraid that his weight will crush her . . .

No. His weight will not crush her.

Abby bites her lower lip to keep from crying out. Abby covers his damp face with kisses, and laughs.

She loves Willem, and that is why she fears him. She fears loving him, for loving is the prelude to loss.

The fear that she will never see him again, one day. This very day, he may disappear from her.

As her father disappeared, and then her mother. For years, she'd had no idea where they were. Falling over the edge of the earth—and gone.

She could not endure it, her solitary life. To live in another is the only life possible for her.

In her ears a low, thrumming sound. Pale

luminous-green buds on trees, thrumming with new life. Murmurous calls of birds. She smiles. She has fallen asleep in the sun.

How long she has been sleeping, she has no idea. An hour? More than an hour? A shadow falls over her.

"Abby?"

Willem speaks softly. He crouches over her, his face strangely creased.

She wants to scream. Willem has grown so old, suddenly . . . How is this possible?

But no, Willem is only frowning. His face is unusually pale. He is so cold that his teeth are chattering—Willem, who is usually perspiring! He touches Abby's shoulder gently, to wake her. Though Abby is certain that she is already awake.

He helps her to her feet. She feels dizzy suddenly, and she clutches at him, panicked.

She cannot summon the words to ask him what he has found in the grasses, in the bank beside the creek. Instead she asks him if he has taken pictures.

"Yes. I did."

Willem pauses, then adds, "I took many pictures."

He has found the skeletons, Abby thinks dreamily.

The knowledge should strike her like a blow to the heart but it does not, unexpectedly. She is still upright. She has overcome the momentary bout of dizziness. *He has found the skeletons. My husband.*

But if this so, what will they do now? What must they do now?

Willem will want to inform the state police. It is clear that he has evidence, he will want to show to the authorities. Not the Shaheen county sheriff's office, but the New York State Police.

Abby will defer to Willem's wishes. Abby understands, she will defer to fate.

It is a strange, suspended moment. Walking slowly, arms around each other's waist, they return to Willem's borrowed car. For the first time, Abby is steadying Willem. She can feel the dampness in his clothing, she can smell his body, which will comfort her all the days of her life.

At the car Willem wipes his eyes. He avoids looking at her.

He is deeply moved, she sees. She'd seen that look in his face, as of exquisite pain, as they were being married by the minister in Willem's church. Other times, when she'd lain in the hospital bed unable to speak. A childish hope comes to her that Willem will siphon the horror from her, absorb it into his soul. For his strength is so much greater than hers.

Willem tells her he didn't disturb anything. Any of the bones, the skulls. Anything washed ashore from the creek.

Willem speaks carefully. As if it were an

everyday matter, a domestic issue, to speak so calmly of *bones, skulls*.

He thinks it might be crucial to let things remain where they are, for law enforcement to examine. Though it has been so many years, not to interfere further. Rotted shreds of clothing, a backpack, a single hiking boot.

What appeared to be rusted handcuffs.

Handcuffs. Abby has never heard this terrible word spoken aloud.

Handcuffs! So it is real, then. It was always real. Not merely a child's nightmare.

Between them, an unspoken alliance. Willem is the only living person to have any awareness of what Abby has felt. Now he knows her intimately.

"One thing I did bring back, Abby. I couldn't leave behind."

His voice quavers, Abby understands that he has something precious for her.

Silently Willem takes her hand in his and opens it, places on the palm a small, badly tarnished ring with a cracked, cloudy-blue opal.

Center Point Large Print
600 Brooks Road / PO Box 1
Thorndike, ME 04986-0001 USA

(207) 568-3717

US & Canada:
1 800 929-9108
www.centerpointlargeprint.com